A LETTER FROM THE

COLONIAL WILLIAMSBURG

FOUNDATION

Maria Rind was a real girl who lived in Williamsburg, Virginia, in the 1770s. Her father, William Rind, ran a printing office and acted as printer for the House of Burgesses. After Mr. Rind died in 1773, his wife, Clementina Rind, took over the family business and editorship of *The Virginia Gazette*. Mrs. Rind was the first woman to operate such an establishment in the colony. Her home and business were both in the Ludwell-Paradise House.

Today, the Ludwell-Paradise House is part of Colonial Williamsburg, a living history museum. The home, along with the rest of Colonial Williamsburg's Historic Area, has been restored to look the way it did at the time of the American Revolution. People in costume tell the story of Virginia's contribution to American independence and show visitors how Williamsburg residents lived during the colonial era.

At Colonial Williamsburg, you can see where Maria lived. You can visit the printing office, post office, and bookbindery to learn about newspapers and books and about how information was obtained and distributed throughout the community. And you can tour the Capitol, where the House of Burgesses decided the fate of Mrs. Rind's contract.

The Colonial Williamsburg Foundation is proud to have worked with Joan Lowery Nixon on the Young Americans series. Staff members met with Mrs. Nixon and identified sources for her research. People at Colonial Williamsburg read each book to make sure it was as accurate as possible, from the way the characters speak, to what they eat, to the clothes they wear. Mrs. Nixon's note at the end of the book tells exactly what we know about Maria, her family, and her friends.

Another way to learn more about the life of Maria Rind and her family and friends is to experience Williamsburg for yourself. A visit to Colonial Williamsburg is a journey to the past—we invite you to join us on that journey and bring history to life.

Cary Carson
Vice President—Research
The Colonial Williamsburg Foundation

Maria's Story
1773

More stories in the

YOUNG AMERICANS

Colonial Williamsburg

SERIES BY JOAN LOWERY NIXON

YOUNG AMERICANS
Colonial Williamsburg

Maria's Story
1773

JOAN LOWERY NIXON

Delacorte Press

Published by
Delacorte Press
an imprint of
Random House Children's Books
a division of Random House, Inc.
1540 Broadway
New York, New York 10036

Colonial Williamsburg is the trade name and registered trademark of the
Colonial Williamsburg Foundation, a not-for-profit organization.

Copyright © 2001 by Joan Lowery Nixon and the Colonial Williamsburg Foundation
Photographs courtesy of the Colonial Williamsburg Foundation
Produced by 17th Street Productions

Visit us on the Web! www.randomhouse.com/kids
Educators and librarians, for a variety of teaching tools, visit us at
www.randomhouse.com/teachers

Library of Congress Cataloging-in-Publication Data
Nixon, Joan Lowery.
    Maria's story, 1773 / Joan Lowery Nixon.
        p. cm.—(Young Americans; 5)
    "Colonial Williamsburg."
    Summary: In Williamsburg, Virginia, two years before the start of the American
Revolution, nine-year-old Maria worries that her mother will lose her contract to publish
official reports and announcements of the British government because she prints anti-
British articles in their family-run newspaper.
    ISBN 0-385-32685-8
    1. Williamsburg (Va.)—History—Colonial period, ca. 1600–1775—Juvenile fiction.
[Williamsburg (Va.)—History—Colonial period, ca. 1600–1775—Fiction.
2. Newspapers—Fiction. 3. Printing—Fiction. 4. Sex role—Fiction.] I. Title.
    PZ7.N65 Mar 2001
[Fic]—dc21

                                                                        2001017495

The text of this book is set in 12-point Minion.
Book design by Patrice Sheridan
Manufactured in the United States of America
August 2001
10 9 8 7 6 5 4 3 2 1
BVG

Contents

Prologue

Stewart Dowling gazed across the empty Market Square. A light mist rose from the wide expanse of grass, and the weather vane on top of the red brick courthouse reflected the rays of the early-morning sun. It was easy to imagine that he was back in the 1700s in colonial Williamsburg.

"Where's Mrs. Otts?" he asked some of the others on his school's field trip. "She said she'd be here early."

Halim Jordan glanced toward Nicholson Street. "Here she comes," he said.

"Good morning, Mrs. Otts," Lori Smith called as Molly Otts entered Market Square.

"Good morning, dearies," Mrs. Otts answered. Dressed in an ankle-length gown and lace-trimmed cap, she swung a large basket of beribboned caps and cocked hats onto the table in her nearby stall. "I see you've come to hear Maria Rind's story."

Chip Hahn ran up, out of breath. "Don't start without me!" he managed to say. "You told us Maria had a secret. Did you tell the secret yet?"

Mrs. Otts smiled. "You'll all learn the secret in due time. But first things first, I always say. 'Tis best you first learn that Maria's father and mother moved to Virginia because the burgesses, including Thomas Jefferson himself, had invited them. Mr. Jefferson asked William Rind to set up a newspaper in Williamsburg that would be more sympathetic to the views of the colonists. Joseph Royle, who published a Williamsburg newspaper called the *Virginia Gazette*, would not print anything critical of the government. He even went so far as to suppress the news of the legislature's resolution protesting the Stamp Act.

"So William Rind rented what is called the Ludwell-Paradise House on Duke of Gloucester Street, set up a press, and began publishing his own *Virginia Gazette*."

"Wait a minute, Mrs. Otts," Stewart said. "How could both newspapers have the same name?"

"At that time," Mrs. Otts answered, "the British insisted that the word *Gazette* had to be used for any publication in which official reports and announcements were printed. The official printing brought printers more revenue than sales of the newspaper alone did, so every printer in the American colonies gave his newspaper the name of his colony plus *Gazette,* hoping to win government contracts."

"Was Mr. Rind successful?" Chip asked.

"He was," Mrs. Otts said. "Mr. Royle died in January, before William and Clementina moved to Williamsburg in 1766. The new owners of his newspaper, John Dixon and Alexander Purdie, were not as one-sided in their views as Mr. Royle, but their newspaper stories about the actions of the Crown and Parliament were mild, so many people felt that the Rind newspaper better reflected the colonists' views. There was competition between the two newspapers, but they both did well."

Chip looked puzzled. "What about Maria's secret?"

Smoothing her skirt, Mrs. Otts said, "Ah, so many questions, so many answers. Let's sit over here on these benches, where we'll be more comfortable, and I'll tell you Maria's story."

With a special smile for Lori and Keisha, she added, "Because Maria was the only daughter in a family with four boys, she had a special bond with both her parents. I believe that during her younger years she was a happy, contented child."

Mrs. Otts paused, and her smile was replaced with a look of sadness. "However, sometimes the peaceful years of childhood come to an end too soon. 'Twas so for nine-year-old Maria when, in 1773, after a long illness, her father died."

Chapter One

Maria Rind had begged to be allowed to go to her father's funeral, but now she was sorry her mother had given in. The Reverend John Dixon's sermon and graveside prayers, the Masonic honors, and the final procession back to the Rind house seemed to be for someone she didn't know, not her father.

Until he became ill, William Rind had been a tall, sturdy man with muscular arms. He could as easily operate the heavy equipment of the printing press as he could swing Maria high into the air. In her mind, Maria could still hear his hearty laughter and her own delighted squealing and see the love and joy in his eyes and in his smile. That was how she wanted to remember her father.

If she could only snuggle next to her mother and

talk about how much she missed Papa, and feel her mother's arms around her . . . but she couldn't.

Clementina Rind had quickly glanced at the friends and acquaintances who were crowding into the Rind home to pay their respects. She had given orders to Dick, their only slave, to serve tea or water to those who wished it, and asked her cousin, John Pinkney, to attend to some of the guests. Then she had turned to Maria, lowering her voice and giving Maria's shoulders a gentle squeeze to reassure her. "We must care for the needs of our guests, daughter," she had said. "I know I can count on you."

A tear rolled down Maria's cheek. She quickly brushed it away and looked around the hall to see if anyone had noticed. Fortunately, at the moment no one seemed to be looking in her direction.

She wished she could shout, "Pray leave us alone and return to your homes! I don't want to curtsy and say polite things to you. I want my mother to hold me and comfort me. I need my mother."

But Maria knew she couldn't possibly do such a shocking thing. She must be a good hostess, as her mother had asked her to be.

Frances Southall, plump with her seventh child, suddenly leaned close to pat Maria's head, startling her. "What a dear, sweet girl you are," Mrs. Southall said. "I know this is a difficult day for you, yet you are a credit to your mother."

Blushing, Maria stammered, "Th-thank you," and remembered to curtsy.

"I know it is difficult for you at a time like this to greet people, but your mother's guests will soon leave," Mrs. Southall whispered.

Maria looked up at her in surprise, wondering if Mrs. Southall could read her mind, but Mrs. Southall was already moving away, offering her arm to an elderly neighbor.

Maria heard her name and turned to see two women nearby eyeing her.

"Maria's a pretty little thing with that dark hair and blue eyes, but she seems much too shy and retiring," said the woman who wore a black cloak.

How can she speak so about me? Maria wondered. *Doesn't she realize that I can hear her?*

"The child resembles her mother," the woman continued, "but she'll never be able to match Mrs. Rind. Look at the dear woman. How very brave and serene she is, in spite of her troubles now and to come."

Troubles to come? What troubles? Maria waited for the woman to explain, but it was the second woman who spoke up.

"You are no doubt correct, Mrs. Miller. I've heard tell that Maria's a practical child, but 'tis obvious she's not as outgoing as her brothers. See how young William stands at his mother's side, greeting the guests? Such a fine little gentleman."

Maria fought to hold back her tears. As she had entered the house after the Masonic procession that escorted them from the church graveyard to their home, she had moved close to her mother and clung to her hand. But William had elbowed her away.

"I'm the eldest. And I'm the man of the family now. This is my place," he'd announced.

Maria had looked beseechingly to her mother for help, but she could see that Clementina—deep in conversation with Ann Pelham, the wife of Bruton Parish organist Peter Pelham—had not heard what William had said.

"Mama?" Maria had begun.

"Mr. Pelham honored us with his beautiful organ music, and we're truly thankful," Mrs. Rind had said to her friend, unaware that Maria was trying to gain her attention.

Maria knew her mother was suffering but had set her feelings aside to greet her guests and put them at ease. Even though Maria was hurt and indignant at what William had said and done, she would never make a scene and cause her mother more pain. She had no choice but to give up her place to William.

Abruptly turning away from the two women who had been discussing her, Maria saw Elizabeth Hay and her sister, Peachy Purdie, enter the house.

Maria felt shy around Mrs. Purdie, who seemed different from her parents' other friends. It was well known that Mrs. Purdie had a mind of her own. While she was still unmarried, she had bought property here in town. And while most young women married in their early twenties, Mrs. Purdie didn't choose to marry until she was thirty-five. Less than a year before, she had married Alexander Purdie, one of the partners who printed the rival *Virginia Gazette*. In writing about the wedding, Maria's father had described Mrs. Purdie in his *Gazette* as "a Lady amiable in her person and of accomplished understanding," so their relationship had always been friendly.

For a moment, Maria's spirits lifted as she saw her best friend, Sarah Hay, squeeze through the doorway past her mother. Maria immediately started toward Sarah, but her five-year-old brother, Charlie, suddenly ran into the hall, weaving around the legs of the many guests. Dashing after him came three-year-old Jemmy, his face contorted in anger.

"Give it to me!" Jemmy yelled.

Maria managed to stop Charlie by grabbing his shoulder. She looked around for Johnny, who was six and usually the ringleader when his brothers were in trouble.

"Where's Johnny?" Maria asked Charlie.

"Outside in the kitchen, looking for something to eat," he answered.

Jemmy leaped at Charlie, grabbing at his shirt. "Give it to me!" he shouted again.

Mrs. Purdie stepped forward and swooped Jemmy into her arms. "Why are you so distressed, little one?" she asked, her voice quiet and soothing.

Jemmy's lower lip curled angrily as he answered, "Charlie took my top."

Charlie glanced up at Maria with a guilty look. He struggled to get away, but her grip was firm. Maria held out her other hand. "I'll take that top," she said.

Reluctantly, Charlie took it from his shirt and gave it to her. "We were only having fun," he said.

"It wasn't fun for Jemmy," Maria told him. She tried to look stern as she handed the top back to her youngest brother. "Remember why our friends are here, Charlie. This is a time to pay respect to Papa. Pray try to be on your best behavior. You, too, Jemmy," she added.

Mrs. Purdie put Jemmy on his feet. As the boys ran off in separate directions, she said to Maria, "You handled that problem very nicely. Your mother would be proud of you."

Sarah, a woebegone look on her face, stepped up and flung her arms around Maria. "I'm so sorry your father died," Sarah said.

Maria clung to Sarah, and this time she couldn't hold back the tears.

Mrs. Hay's arms encircled the girls, and Maria leaned close, feeling the way a baby bird must feel with his mother's comforting wings around him.

"Why don't you two visit upstairs?" Mrs. Hay suggested.

"I must help my mother," Maria answered, but she felt herself being shepherded toward the stairway, and she didn't try to resist.

"I'll take your place," Mrs. Hay insisted, so Maria picked up her skirt and ran upstairs, Sarah following.

Maria's tears stemmed not only from longing for her father but also from embarrassment at not fulfilling her mother's wishes. Her mother hadn't given in to tears. Why couldn't Maria be strong like that?

The words Mrs. Miller had spoken suddenly pushed again into Maria's mind: *How very brave and serene she is, in spite of her troubles now and to come.*

Maria turned to Sarah, who had sat next to her, an arm around her shoulders, waiting patiently until she had stopped crying. Sarah's father had died just three years before. Maybe she'd know what the woman had meant.

Telling Sarah only those few words of the conversation, Maria asked, "What did Mrs. Miller mean about troubles to come?"

Sarah shook her head. "I have no idea. I remember my mother speaking with Uncle Matthew about a will and papers to sign. Since Uncle Matthew is an attorney, he was able to help her with the matter."

Sarah thought a moment, then added, "Troubles? 'Twas certainly a strange thing to say. Why don't you ask your mother? She might know what Mrs. Miller was talking about."

"I think I shall," Maria answered. Surely people would leave the house soon and there would be time to sit with her mother and talk.

However, the sun was setting before the last guests had gone to their own homes, leaving behind food for the Rinds' supper. Maria couldn't eat. She picked at the cold vegetables on her plate, unable to take even a mouthful.

She knew that the boys and Isaac Collins, her father's apprentice, were grief-stricken, too, but their feelings didn't seem to affect their appetites. They quickly devoured a game pie and a rich custard.

Isaac was a shy lad, who tended to duck his head and stare at his toes after the few times he'd added to the conversation. But Maria understood how Isaac felt. Sometimes she felt just as shy and quiet herself.

Cousin John Pinkney, who for many years had lived with the Rinds, pushed his chair back from the table, asked to be excused, and announced that he had plans to visit friends for the evening.

Clementina nodded agreement as if she were only half-listening, so Cousin John buttoned up his blue coat, donned his cocked hat, and left the house.

Cousin John was a pleasant person, Maria thought. He was likable and tried to get along with everyone. She had never seen him in a bad mood. For many years he had worked in the printing office with her father, and she wondered if now he would take over the business from her mother.

No, he can't, she thought with a sinking feeling. John was a capable worker, but he was not as clever as her father. Papa had had a knack for choosing interesting and exciting items for his newspaper, and he'd had many loyal readers who wouldn't miss a single weekly issue.

Young William said, "Cousin John is going to Southall's tavern, Mama, to visit with his friends."

Clementina laid a hand over William's, giving it a

loving squeeze. "I know, child," she said. "Cousin John's friends are good men, and they will give him the companionship he needs."

Frowning in disgust, William said, "All they seem to talk about is our governor, Lord Dunmore, and what a mean, unlikable person he is."

"Unfortunately, 'tis true," Clementina said.

Maria gave her brother a sharp look. "How do you know what Cousin John and his friends talk about?" she asked.

William pulled his hand away and jumped up from his chair. "I have friends to see, too," he said.

Clementina raised her head. "William—" she began, but William ran from the house, banging the door behind him.

Maria stood and asked, "Shall I go after him, Mama?" She was willing, even though William, a year older than she, was taller and stronger and could easily outrun her.

"No, daughter," Clementina said. "William needs to be with his friends, too. We all need . . ."

As her mother's voice broke, Maria picked up the bowl of vegetables. "I will see if Dick has had enough to eat. Then I'll put away the dishes and tuck Johnny and Charlie and Jemmy into their beds."

" 'Tis not time for bed," Johnny complained.

"Not nearly," Charlie added.

Jemmy slid out of his chair and climbed under the table. "I'm not going to bed," he announced.

"You won't be able to hear a story if you're under the table," Clementina told him.

"What story?" Jemmy crawled halfway out and looked up at his mother.

"A story you like, about the lion with a sore paw."

"Who eats people," Charlie added.

"Does not!" Jemmy said.

Maria scraped the scraps from the plates and carried them to the outside kitchen. She would heat water to wash them the next morning when it was light.

As Maria folded their dining table, putting it against the wall, she heard the soft voice of her mother in the next room as she told the story. She knew that her mother would be seated in the big wing chair, Charlie at her feet, Johnny leaning on one arm, and little Jemmy in her lap.

With an agonizing burst of jealousy, Maria thought, *I wish it were me. I need my mother! I need her right now!*

Chapter Two

It was difficult to be patient, but finally Maria and her mother had coaxed the little boys up to the chamber they shared and now, tucked into their trundle beds, they had fallen asleep.

As they returned to the hall, Maria flung herself at her mother, hugging her tightly. "Mama, I'm sorry I didn't do as you asked," she said.

Clementina enfolded Maria in her arms. "What didn't you do?" she questioned.

"I wasn't strong, like you," Maria answered. "I cried. Then I stopped greeting our guests and went upstairs with Sarah." Again she said, "Mama, I'm sorry."

"There is nothing to be sorry for, dear child," Clementina told her. "I am very proud of you for being such a brave girl. I understand how much you miss your father."

Her mother's words broke off in a sob. Maria quickly looked up to see that her mother was crying.

"Oh, Mama!" she said in anguish. "I didn't mean to make you cry."

" 'Tis not your doing," Clementina quickly answered. A wet cheek brushed Maria's forehead as her mother bent to kiss her. "I miss your father, too."

Again they hugged, Maria burying her face in the warmth of her mother's shoulder.

When they stepped apart, Clementina pulled a handkerchief from her pocket and wiped her eyes. Smiling at Maria, she said, "It's been a long, exhausting day, dear one. It's time for you to go to bed."

Now is not the time to ask Mama about troubles to come, Maria decided. She kissed her mother good night and went above stairs.

Just before she fell asleep, she heard the murmur of her brother William's voice as he returned home. *Mama was so exhausted, and now she can retire,* Maria thought. Immediately she fell asleep.

Sometime during the early morning hours, however, Maria awoke, her empty stomach rumbling. At supper she hadn't felt like eating. Now she was truly hungry.

Dressed only in her shift, Maria stole down the

stairs, hoping to find something to eat in the pantry. To her surprise, she glimpsed the flicker of candle-light in the room in which the family ate its meals. Who besides her was up at this hour?

Cautiously, Maria peeked in at the door and saw her mother, bent over the table in a pool of dim candlelight, writing with quill pen and ink.

"Mama?" Maria asked in surprise. "What are you doing?"

Startled, Clementina jerked upright. "Oh! It's you, Maria," she said. She leaned back in her chair, closed her eyes, and rubbed the bridge of her nose. "At the moment I'm writing an account of your papa's funeral for the *Gazette*," she answered. Her voice grew stronger as she added, "And when I have finished, I must give some thought to what else will go into the next issue of the newspaper."

Clementina rubbed her tired eyes again. "We must print the next issue of the *Gazette* on time. We cannot afford to miss a Thursday."

"*You* will do this, Mama?" Maria asked in amazement. "*You* will do what Papa did?"

"Yes, I will," Clementina answered firmly. She paused, then smiled and held out her arms to Maria. "But I will need your help."

With a burst of excitement, Maria ran to stand before her mother. "I will do anything, Mama," she eagerly promised. "I can learn to set type, as apprentice Isaac does. I may not be tall enough or strong enough to lift the presses, but with Dick's help, or Cousin John's—"

"Maria, lamb, listen to me," Clementina said as she gently placed her fingertips on Maria's lips. "Fortunately, while your father was ill, I assisted him enough to know what needs to be done. We will have Cousin John's and Isaac's help, and Dick to do the heavy work. I have asked your brother William to learn the trade from Cousin John and from me. William will work at our side."

"You asked *William*?" Maria whispered in shock. "Mama, William has always been a prankster. He does things he shouldn't, then makes people laugh so he won't be scolded. I have heard Papa tell him more than once that he was not behaving re—respon—"

"Responsibly," Clementina said. "I know, but now—"

"Even now, Mama, you cannot count on William to be at hand when he's needed."

Clementina sighed and said, "William is quick to learn, and he reads and writes well. We spoke about our new situation when he returned home tonight, and he solemnly promised me he would put aside boyish games and work at each job until it is completed."

Clementina continued to tell Maria what she had planned, but Maria no longer listened. As her face burned with hurt and shame, she could only repeat over and over to herself the words her mother had spoken: *William is quick to learn, and he reads and writes well.* That is why he and not Maria had been chosen to help at the printing office.

Her mother's voice broke into Maria's thoughts. "Maria? Are you woolgathering again? Or are you listening to me?"

"I—I'm listening now, Mama."

"Very well. I'll tell you again. I'll need your help with the little boys—especially with Jemmy. And even though we've only recently begun your training with household chores and cooking, I'm counting on a great deal of your help with these tasks as well. Without you I don't see how I can manage to care for the little boys and the household, write and print the *Gazette,* and do the government printing for which your father was awarded a contract."

Still hurt and disappointed by her mother's announcement, Maria blurted out the secret she had tried to keep from everyone, even Sarah, her best friend. "Are you asking me to do household chores instead of work with you on the *Gazette* because I am slow to learn to read?"

Her mother looked distressed. "Maria, dear, with

your father so ill and needing care, I neglected your studies. That is not your fault. And it is not the reason I have chosen William to help me at the printing office. Surely you understand that household work and the care of little children are jobs that women were born to do."

Reluctantly, Maria said, "Yes, Mama, but—"

Clementina ignored Maria's interruption and continued. "Your father had always intended that William would one day apprentice with him and learn the printer's trade. William is merely beginning his apprenticeship early. He will be helping me while he learns skills that will allow him to support a family when he is grown."

Maria knew she should agree with her mother, but it was hard to do. *I would love to learn how to write and print newspaper stories,* she thought. *Mama often helped Papa in the printing office. I could help, too.*

Clementina reached out to hold Maria's shoulders. Gazing earnestly into her eyes, Clementina said, "We have many difficulties ahead of us."

"Troubles, Mama?" Was this what the woman in the black cloak had meant?

For a moment Clementina seemed puzzled. Then she said, "The tasks ahead are not what I would have chosen for us, but I would not call them troubles. I'd rather call them blessings, because we own a business that can provide food and shelter for us. You are a good, practical child. You understand what must be done. Will you help me?"

Maria sighed. That she was practical was true. And what her mother was asking her to do did make sense. With an ache in her heart, she realized that her father would want her above all to be an obedient daughter. Wistfully, Maria leaned to kiss her mother's cheek. "I will do anything you ask of me, Mama," she answered.

"Thank you, Maria," her mother said. As she turned to pick up the quill pen, she added, "If I hope to finish in time, I must return to work."

Maria left and searched the pantry, cutting herself a slice of bread and a piece of cheese. While she munched, she thought over all that her mother had told her. Operating the printing office was apparently not one of the troubles—perhaps not to her mother. But her new chores were a trouble to Maria. She knew that taking care of the household was important, but she wanted to do more than that. She wanted to help her mother with her work.

"If only I could read as well as William," Maria said aloud to herself. "Then I could help Mama with the newspaper in my free time. William is not the only one she can rely on. Somehow I'll learn to read so I can work at the press, too."

Chapter Three

The next few days were difficult for all the members of the Rind family. There was little time for Maria to mourn her father. She constantly struggled with the household tasks her mother had never found time to teach her to do. And preparing both early afternoon dinners and simple evening suppers was a frightening chore, with only her mother's hurried instructions to go by. To make Maria's job even harder, she had to tend to her three younger brothers, who seemed to have made up their minds to cause trouble.

Although the printing office took up half of the lower floor of their home, Maria soon learned that she could not interrupt her mother, no matter what problem she might face.

"Mama," she cried as she opened the door that

connected the office and the family's living quarters, "I scorched the milk for the rice pudding you told me to make. I left the pan on the fire and went to tend to Jemmy. Now there's not enough milk left to scald more. What shall I do?"

Clementina looked up impatiently from the tray of type. "Set the pudding aside. We will have plain boiled rice with a bit of butter. Now, leave us, please, Maria. We're very busy."

William leaned around Cousin John to grin wickedly at Maria. "Scorched milk? What a waste!" he said in a shocked voice.

Maria backed away and silently closed the door, but soon Johnny and Charlie, with shouts and laughter, began to tussle.

"Stop that this instant!" Maria ordered. "You are rolling around the floor like little animals!"

Not only did the boys ignore her, but Jemmy leapt on his brothers, yelling and laughing.

"I said stop!" Maria shouted. She grabbed the back of Charlie's collar and tried to pull him to his feet, but the collar ripped. Maria, the torn collar still in her grip, lost her balance, plopping down on the hard wooden floor.

She stared in shock at the collar. "Now see what you've done!" she cried.

Her brothers untangled themselves and looked at her.

"I told you to behave yourselves," Maria scolded.

"You aren't our mother," Johnny grumbled.

Charlie nodded in agreement. "So you can't tell us what to do."

"Mama told me to take care of you."

Jemmy complained, "We were only playing, Maria. Mama lets us play."

Charlie frowned at his shirt collar. "Mama doesn't tear our clothes," he said.

"Or yell at us," Johnny added.

Maria slowly got to her feet and opened the door to the printing office. "Mama," she said. "I can't do anything with the boys. They won't behave."

Clementina straightened and wiped the back of one hand across her forehead. "It's up to you to make them behave," she said impatiently.

"I accidentally tore Charlie's shirt."

"Then mend it with your smallest, most careful stitches." Clementina sighed and added, "Maria, I don't want you to open that door again. Each interruption delays our work. You will have to handle every problem yourself, without my help. Do you understand me, daughter?"

William's grin grew broader, and he snickered.

Maria tried to gulp down the lump that rose in her throat. "I'm sorry, Mama," she whispered, but her mother had already turned away from her and was instructing Dick to ink the forme, the pages of type in the press.

Slowly, Maria shut the door. Even though she wanted to run upstairs to her bedchamber, fling herself on the bed, and give in to tears, she was practical enough to realize that her mother was right. She must handle all problems herself—beginning with her little brothers.

She opened her parents' desk and took out a dozen sheets of paper. These were broadsides that had been printed or sheets that had been rejected.

"I'm going to make a ship," Maria said. She began folding the paper.

"You can't make a ship out of paper," Johnny argued.

Maria didn't answer. She just kept smoothing the paper and folding it.

Charlie squatted down in front of her. "How do you make a ship?" he asked.

"Like this," Maria said. She took a second sheet of paper and made the first fold for Charlie. Then she held out her own sheet of paper. "Now we fold it here . . . and here . . . yes, just like that."

"I want to make a ship, too," Johnny said.

Maria handed him a sheet of paper and showed him how to make the first fold.

Jemmy climbed into Maria's lap. "I want a ship," he said.

"This one's for you," Maria told him. She finished her ship and gave it to Jemmy. Then she helped Johnny and Charlie with theirs and put Jemmy on the floor.

Rising to her feet, she said, "The hall is the James River, and these are ships that have come from England to bring cloth and paper, paint and glass, and many other things the Virginia colonists need. Merchants will then fill the ships with tobacco to send back to England."

"Where are the ships with British soldiers?" Johnny asked.

"You can make them," Maria told him. "You can make all the ships you like. Here is more paper."

As the boys worked busily, Maria went out to the kitchen. It was time to mix dough for johnnycakes, put hot coals under the Dutch oven, and wash a pan of carrots to go with the boiled chicken they'd eat for their main meal in the early afternoon.

Dick had laid logs and kindling in the fireplace, so it was not hard for Maria to start a fire. But once it was blazing, she stood without moving in the middle of the kitchen floor, clenching her hands together in panic. What was she supposed to do next?

How should she boil the chicken? Its head, feet, and feathers had been removed, but was she supposed to plop it whole into the pan of water? Should she cut it in big chunks or little chunks? And for how long should she cook it? Her mother hadn't told her, and she absolutely couldn't open the door to the printing office and ask her. Maria sighed with relief as she saw her mother come through the kitchen door.

"I'll start the cooking, daughter, but you must tend it until it is done."

A loud wail from Jemmy caused Maria to pick up her skirts and run back to the house.

Johnny, shouting with laughter, was holding off Jemmy, who yelled and sobbed in anger.

Maria picked up Jemmy, trying to soothe him. "I won't know what's wrong until you stop crying and tell me," she said.

As Jemmy struggled to curb his tears, Charlie said, "I'll tell you what happened. Pirates sank Jemmy's ship."

"Pirates?"

Quickly Johnny said, "You told us we could make all the ships we like, so we made some pirate ships."

Maria groaned. *How has Mama managed to take care of these three? And how am I going to manage?* she wondered. It was too much to ask of anyone.

Jemmy had stopped wailing, so Maria put him back on the floor. "Give Jemmy back his ship," she said. "No pirates, no fighting, no sinking ships. Those are the rules."

"Pirates don't obey rules," Charlie said.

"We don't have to do what you say," Johnny began, but Maria took a step forward, glaring at him.

"Oh, yes, you do," she said. "Mama said so. I'll tell her what you just said and see what she has to say about it when she comes for the afternoon meal."

The afternoon meal! Everyone would arrive at the dining room to eat before long and she had not even given one pot a stir since her mother got the cooking started. Maria turned and ran back out to the kitchen.

Later, as Dick served the bowls of chicken, vegetables, and rice to the family, Clementina smiled at Maria. "Thank you, daughter, for preparing this lovely meal."

William made a face. "It's not lovely. The carrots are mushy, the chicken is tough as a harness strap, and there's no sauce to put over it."

"There's not supposed to be sauce," Maria said. "I don't know how to make sauce."

Cousin John spoke up, his voice hearty. "I, for one, like my chicken well done and chewy. Good job, Maria."

29

"Cousin John's just trying to be polite," Johnny said. "The chicken has no more flavor than a chunk of wood."

Charlie elbowed Johnny, nearly pushing him out of his chair. "Bet you never tasted a chunk of wood in your whole life."

Clementina reached over to pat Maria's arm. "A lesson in making sauces is one we'll have to have soon," she said. "It is my fault that I forgot to remind you to salt the meat." She glanced at the nearly full bowl of chicken pieces. "This evening you can cut up the leftover chicken, add the pieces to the carrots, and put them in the soup you'll make from the water you boiled the chicken in."

"Oh," Maria said in despair. She had disappointed her mother again. "I didn't know I was supposed to save the water, Mama. I—I threw it out."

Clementina closed her eyes for just a moment, and everyone at the table was silent, wondering what she was going to say. But she opened her eyes and smiled at Maria. "We both have much to learn, daughter," she said. "We will learn together."

She looked around the table, her eyes resting for a moment on each of the boys. "I know we will have help and cooperation from William, Johnny, Charlie, and Jemmy," she said.

Jemmy smiled and looked earnestly at Clementina. "Papa said I am always a good lad, Mama," he told her.

Clementina hesitated for only a moment. "Your papa was right," she said.

The small clock on the mantel chimed three times, and Clementina pushed her chair away from the table. "Time to get back to the presses," she announced. Cousin John immediately stood and joined her as she walked across the stair hall to the printing office.

Maria watched William slowly get to his feet.

He looked up, seeing that her eyes were on him, and frowned. "Being a printer is hard, tiring work," he said.

"But it's interesting work," Maria countered.

"How would you know?" William grumbled. "You have the easy part, just doing household work."

Easy? A lot he knows! "I could do the writing and printing chores," Maria said. "I could do them as well—even better—than you."

William laughed. "You say you can write? When you can barely read? That's very funny."

Maria's face grew hot with both embarrassment and anger. She opened her mouth to retort, but Clementina called from the printing office, "William? Where are you?"

As William ran to answer, Maria gripped the back

of one of the dining chairs. She'd show William he was wrong, and she knew just how to do it.

If William could learn to read well, then so could she. Even if her mother had no time to continue her lessons, she'd practice. She'd make the time for study. She'd prove to her mother that she could read well, too. Then perhaps someday her mother would say, "Maria, you can take my place in the printing office today." Or, "Maria, you can take William's place."

Oh, yes! That would be even better. Maria smiled as she scraped the plates and carried them outside to the kitchen. She would do it! She made a solemn promise to herself.

Chapter Four

On Thursday morning, while Maria was trying to settle an argument between Charlie and Johnny, Clementina walked in from the printing office.

She wiped her ink-stained hands on a rag, removed her leather printer's apron, and announced, "The *Gazette* has been printed and delivered, Maria, thanks to your good help."

She smiled as she raised her voice over the clamor set up by the boys, who rushed to greet her. "I included an invitation for new subscribers and a request that those who have submitted items that have already been printed pay their bills. With prayer and hard work and the payment due us under the contract your father obtained for government printing, our little family will survive."

Clementina dropped into the nearest chair. Jemmy dived into her lap. Maria ran to hug her mother.

"I'm so glad you'll be our mother again," Maria said. "The children have been a worrisome handful, and—"

Clementina freed a hand to stroke the hair back from Maria's forehead, tucking it under her cap. "I didn't stop being your mother," she said. "I simply had to take your father's place in the printing office. I know I am asking you to make a great sacrifice. I will help with the larger household tasks as much as I can and teach you more things. But we must continue what we have all been doing, daughter, so we can keep printing the *Gazette* each week. Do you understand?"

At that moment Charlie jumped on Johnny, pummeling him. As Clementina attempted to rise to stop the argument, Jemmy flung his arms around his mother's neck and yelled.

Can't Mama and I have a moment's peace? Exasperated, Maria tugged Charlie away from Johnny, stood him on his feet, and marched him to the corner, where she plopped him down, facing the wall. "Sit there for ten minutes by the clock," she ordered.

Charlie glared at Maria. "Mama!" he shouted.

"Do as your sister tells you," Clementina said firmly. "Maria is in charge."

Charlie frowned even more as he turned to Maria. "Johnny took my whirligig. He won't give it back."

"Oh, yes, he will," Maria said. She looked firmly at Johnny, who thought only a moment before he handed the toy to Maria.

"When your ten minutes is up, you may have your whirligig," she said to Charlie.

Clementina smiled her approval at Maria, who was glad she had pleased her mother. However, she couldn't help feeling a bit rebellious. She needed her mother herself and had no wish to become a substitute mother to her noisy, active brothers.

Cousin John, buttoning his waistcoat, entered the hall, but there was no sign of William.

"Where is William?" Maria asked.

"William was asked by one of the clerks to personally deliver a copy of the *Gazette* to him at the courthouse," Clementina answered.

Cousin John rolled his eyes. "Which William will do, knowing he'll be given a tip."

"Now, cousin," Clementina began.

But John had more to say. "William is not the most dependable of boys. Set him a task, and you're fortunate if he begins it within the half hour."

"John, remember that William is but a child," Clementina said. "He has much to learn."

"Hmph!" Cousin John said. "When I was a lad we quickly learned to mind our p's and q's."

Maria's sympathy was with her brother. She loved him in spite of his teasing and boasting. But she still regretted that *she* couldn't be the one her mother asked to work in the printing office.

William returned in time for the family's afternoon meal. All during the meal, William bragged about the work he had done in helping to print the newspaper. And he had a great deal to say about comments some readers had made.

"There were many who noticed that your name replaced Papa's as printer of the *Gazette*, Mama. Some spoke their approval. One of the justices even told me I was a good lad from a good family as he gave me a coin."

William chuckled and added, "Later, I overheard an old gentleman. He sat on a bench in front of the King's Arms Tavern as his daughters read some of the *Gazette* aloud to him. He grumbled that the newspaper had too much of a woman's influence in it.

"One of his daughters said, ' 'Tis good to see in the newspaper tributes to women in verse and riddle. They appeal to women.' But he pounded the end of his cane on the ground and shouted, 'There is never a good reason to appeal to women!' "

Cousin John laughed loudly, but Clementina

looked intently at William. "What were you doing in front of the King's Arms Tavern?" she asked.

Maria didn't listen to William's answer. Instead, she pictured William at the courthouse, being complimented by one of the justices. And in her mind she saw him strolling Duke of Gloucester Street, free to watch what was going on and enjoy bits of conversations. With all her might she fought against the envy that burned within her chest. If only she were a boy, instead of a girl . . . If she were the eldest . . . If she could read with skill . . .

I will read well, she promised herself again. *I've been practicing, whenever I've had the chance. 'Tis difficult, but—*

She felt a hand placed on her shoulder, and she heard her mother say, "Dear daughter, I fear you've been woolgathering again. The others have all left the table."

"I'm sorry, Mama," Maria said as she quickly stumbled to her feet. "There is so much to think about."

Clementina put an arm around Maria's shoulders. "Perhaps 'tis time to give you something else to think about. I have made a short list of things I need from John Greenhow's store. A spool of white thread, a skein of knitting wool, two buttons to replace the ones lost from Charlie's breeches, and a small packet of ground cinnamon. I should write them down, but . . ."

As Clementina hesitated, Maria said quickly, " 'Tis no matter, Mama. I can remember your list."

Smiling, Clementina asked, "Would you like to go shopping for me?"

Upstairs there was a loud thump, and Charlie let out a shout.

"Oh, yes, Mama!" Maria cried, eager to leave the house, even to run an errand.

Clementina put her hands on Maria's shoulders. "Dear daughter," she said, "there is no reason why you cannot ask Sarah to visit on an occasional afternoon and keep you company. You needn't spend all your time on chores."

"But the boys—"

"Sarah might like to help you keep them occupied. She also has brothers. And don't forget, your brothers have chores to do, too."

"Thank you, Mama," Maria said. She eagerly ran to get her cloak.

During the next three weeks, Maria became more used to the new pattern of her life. She remembered to salt the meat, to test the vegetables so that they were not overcooked, and never to leave a pan on the fire unattended.

She gave her brothers small tasks to keep them

busy and took them for long walks to use up some of their energy. Twice she entertained Sarah, proud that she had set a pretty table, even though her johnny-cakes had crumbled at a touch. Maria and Sarah simply popped the broken cakes into their mouths and licked their fingers with delight because no adults were present to tell them to mind their manners.

And while there was still light, Maria always made time to study the Bible and simple books for beginners that her mother had used when she first began to teach her letters and words.

Maria could recognize most of the letters of the alphabet, but strung together in words they became a strange, frightening jumble. She scowled at the pages as she tried to sound out the words. William could read well. Sarah, too. So Maria thought there was no reason why she herself couldn't become a good reader if she tried hard enough.

Maria refused to give up hope that someday she would become a good reader. How proud her mother would be of her! Maria studied the issues of her mother's *Virginia Gazette,* even attempting to read the advertisements, obituaries, lists of ships' arrivals and departures, and advertisements reporting runaway slaves. She knew that every word that appeared in the newspaper was first written down before it was set in type, so she *must* learn to read and write. But try as she might, Maria couldn't make sense of the letters. Why was learning so difficult?

Maria occasionally heard her mother speaking to Cousin John about the Tea Act, which Parliament had passed in May. Clementina's voice was filled with outrage as she complained about the favoritism Parliament had shown to the East India Company, preventing its bankruptcy by removing export taxes on its tea, allowing its agents to undersell other tea merchants. Occasionally Clementina included an article in the *Gazette* complaining about the taxes on tea and urging her readers to give up drinking it.

On Thursday, September 23, on her weekly trip to Mr. Greenhow's store, Maria quietly waited for her turn to make her small purchases. She looked forward to giving her order to Mr. Greenhow. He always greeted her with great friendliness, asking about the well-being of her mother and brothers.

Ahead of Maria at the counter stood a woman whose slave stepped up to gather the woman's purchases. In a loud voice the woman checked off her selections, saying to Mr. Greenhow, "And *tea*. I would not be without my tea. Can you imagine that Clementina Rind ordering us not to drink tea? As if I would pack away my precious china tea set! I have a good mind to stop reading her *Gazette*."

Maria stiffened as she recognized that the voice

belonged to Mrs. Miller, who had just as firmly pointed out Maria's shortcomings after her father's funeral. *She is not being fair,* Maria thought indignantly. *Mama did not order anyone to stop drinking tea. She merely suggested that people protest the tax by not serving tea. It was not the amount of the tax. It was the principal of the thing.*

Elizabeth Geddy, the wife of silversmith James Geddy, spoke up. Her voice was a quiet contrast to Mrs. Miller's. "I like to read the many fine articles in Mrs. Rind's newspaper," Mrs. Geddy said. "Did you see the recent printing of excellent recipes for those suffering from the flux?"

Mrs. Miller shook her head. "No one in my family has had the flux, and if they did, I would simply put them in bed and dose them with barley water."

"Last week in Mistress Rind's *Gazette,* she wrote in detail about the opening of our new public hospital for persons of unsound mind," someone else said, "whereas the other *Gazette* gave the hospital but short mention."

Scowling, Mrs. Miller said, " 'Tis all well and good, but mark my words, Clementina Rind will someday find herself in trouble for giving too much space to colonial grievances against the Crown."

Mrs. Geddy answered, "She is but following her newspaper's motto. At the top of each front page is

41

printed, 'Open to ALL PARTIES but influenced by NONE.' To my mind, she speaks for Virginians, as her husband before her did."

Mrs. Miller tucked in her chin and looked down her nose at Mrs. Geddy. "I do not consider myself simply a colonial," she said. "I am British through and through and a loyal subject of our good King George." Turning abruptly, she swept from the store, her slave following.

Mr. Greenhow bent over the counter to smile at Maria. "How does your good mother today?" he asked. "And your brothers?"

As Maria smiled in return and answered Mr. Greenhow's polite questions, she couldn't help wondering if there were many others who also disliked her mother's *Gazette* because her mother did not hesitate to air colonists' grievances against the Crown.

Mrs. Miller had spoken of troubles to come. Would this be part of the trouble—that more people would favor the rival *Gazette* because of her mother's strong views?

As she waited for her parcel to be wrapped, Maria shivered. What were the troubles to come? When and how could she find out?

Chapter Five

Maria returned home to discover everyone in her family—even Cousin John—seated at the dining table. Her mother glanced up from the writing papers that lay in front of her and nodded to Maria.

"We waited for you," she said.

As Maria slipped into her chair, she asked, "Waited? For what, Mama?"

Clementina, her face pale except for the dark shadows under her eyes, took a deep breath before she spoke, her voice trembling. "I have just been informed that on Monday your father's personal estate will be inventoried and appraised by law."

"What does that mean, Mama?" Johnny asked.

Clementina's shoulders drooped. "Dear children," she said, "your father did not see fit to leave a will, since he owned no land to leave his sons. But he died owing debts, which must be paid. Since we cannot pay all the debts, our possessions will have to be sold at public auction. The court has appointed appraisers who will come into our home and printing office and decide what everything we own is worth."

Maria gasped in shock, and William cried, "Everything, Mama?"

A tear rolled down Clementina's cheek. She wiped it away before she answered, her voice bitter, "Everything, son, except what a widow is usually allowed to keep—her bed and a cooking pot."

"Oh, dear. Oh, dear," Cousin John murmured over and over. His face turned red, and he nervously rubbed his nose with the knuckles of one fist.

"What about our other beds?" Maria asked. "Surely we will not be told to sell the beds in which we sleep."

Clementina seemed to find it hard to speak. Finally, she answered by pointing to the papers before her and saying, "Our printing equipment and most of the household furniture and kitchen equipment, sheets, pillowcases, warming pans, dishes, tea sets . . . My own newspaper will carry a notice of the public sale, which is set for October second."

Her voice broke, and she murmured, "They will take even my silver spoons."

Not Mama's four precious silver spoons! Maria thought. Her grandmother had given the spoons to her mother, and Maria knew that her mother had planned to give them to her someday. How could the deputy sheriff settling the estate force them to sell the silver spoons?

Maria took a deep breath to steady herself. There was much more to worry about than silver spoons. They were only material things, and material things could be replaced.

The printing equipment, however, was different. Mama must not lose it. How could she print the newspaper? Or fulfill the government contract for printing, which Papa was so pleased to have been granted?

Charlie piped up. "Mama, you will have a bed, but where will the rest of us sleep?"

Clementina shook her head, burying her face in her hands. "I cannot think," she murmured. "I cannot think."

Jemmy cried out, "Mama, is some man going to come into our house and take our toys?"

"No! I won't let him!" Johnny shouted, and Jemmy began to sob.

Clementina pulled Jemmy onto her lap and tried to soothe him, begging the other boys to be quiet.

Cousin John raised his voice above the hubbub. He took a folded sheet of paper from the pocket of his waistcoat, opened it, and said, "There is more, madam. This is an advertisement that was brought into the office a scant hour ago with a request that it be printed in our next issue of the *Gazette*. I had not had time to show it to you. Do you wish me to read it?"

"Pray do so," Clementina said. "Hush, children, and listen."

Cousin John said, "This notice announces for sale several tenements in Williamsburg belonging to a William Lee of London, one being—" He cleared his throat and read aloud, " 'the brick house on the Main Street where Mrs. Rind lives.' "

"The house we are renting is now for sale? What else can happen to us?" Clementina bent her head to Jemmy's shoulder, clung to him, and shook with silent tears.

So all this must be what Mrs. Miller meant when she talked of the troubles to come, Maria thought. While her mother's news was terrifying, for some reason Maria did not panic, as her brothers had done. She felt a strange relief that she had finally learned the answer to the question that had worried her ever since the day of her father's funeral. And with that relief came a clear thought.

"Mama," she said. "We do not have to sell everything."

William, his face puffy and red from crying, glared at Maria. "You don't know anything about this," he said. "You're only a girl."

"There must be a way Mama can keep the printing equipment."

"Do you think the courts will care that it means our livelihood?" William countered.

Maria turned away from William and raised her voice. "Mama," she said, "pray listen to me! Papa was government printer. I have heard you speak of a contract. How long is Papa's contract with the burgesses?"

Clementina raised her head. Slowly, she sat a little straighter. "The contract covers many more months. It lasts until spring of next year," she answered. "Why do you ask?"

"Because, Mama," Maria told her, "if you have a contract with the government for printing, then you must have use of the equipment with which to carry out the contract. Is that not right?"

Clementina's eyes widened. "Why, yes," she said. "Of course. That is a strong argument I could make to the court. Perhaps even the church vestry might support my plea, because if I cannot care for my children and myself, they will have to find places for our destitute family."

"One more thing, Mama," Maria said. "Moving to another house would interfere with finishing some of the contract. If this house is sold, perhaps some of the justices will use their influence to urge the new owner to allow us to continue living here."

Clementina squared her shoulders, set Jemmy on the floor, and stood, smoothing down her skirt. "Dear little daughter," she said, "if I had not allowed myself to become so upset, I would have seen what you clearly observed. Thank you for your good, practical sense."

Maria, warmed by her mother's praise, smiled in answer. Her mother needed her. She truly needed her—and in a very important way.

"Will they still take my bed?" Charlie asked.

"We might lose most of our household goods, but we will not give up. There are people among our friends and neighbors to whom I can talk. Even lawyers, justices, and burgesses have families. I am sure if there is a way for us to keep our household and business together, we will soon learn of it."

"Good for you, Mama!" William cried.

Charlie looked back and forth from his older brother and sister to his mother. Bewildered, he asked again, "But where will we all sleep?"

Maria picked him up. "You will have a place to sleep," she told him. "I promise."

In spite of her brave words, Maria couldn't help

being frightened, too. How could she possibly keep this promise?

Clementina rested a hand on Maria's shoulder. "I am going to wash my face and change my clothes," she said. "There are people I must see—people who can lend me support."

Maria smiled encouragement. She wondered who her mother would ask for help in keeping her printing equipment. Perhaps Thomas Jefferson, who had invited her father to publish a newspaper in Williamsburg. Or perhaps some of the many burgesses who wished the colonists' side to continue to be told in a Virginia newspaper.

But a short while later, as she heard her mother leave the house, Maria felt another shiver of fear. Her mother had to succeed! She had to!

Clementina returned much later—long after Johnny, Charlie, and Jemmy had been tucked into their beds. Although she drooped with exhaustion, she told Maria, William, and Cousin John that she had found the support she needed. She had been advised by two burgesses, both attorneys, that a way might be found for her to buy back some of her furniture and the printing equipment. In the meantime, the courts would most likely allow her to keep the printing equipment so that she could fulfill her government contract.

She added, "At least until May of next year, when the House of Burgesses meets again. Then we may need to compete with Mr. Alexander Purdie and his partner, Mr. John Dixon, who wish to be given the contract, too."

Clementina gave a long, exhausted sigh. " 'Tis late, dear ones. We should all be in bed. Tomorrow we'll have much to do."

Maria obediently climbed the stairs behind her mother. One problem had been overcome, but that was not enough. She dreaded what would happen on Monday, when the appraisers would arrive to inventory the Rinds' household goods.

Mrs. Hay and Sarah arrived at the Rinds' home just as the sky turned light. They carried aprons, brooms, and a hamper filled with apples, bread, cheese, gingerbread squares, and drinking cups for water. "We are here to help," Mrs. Hay said simply.

"Dear Elizabeth, you are a friend to be treasured," Clementina said.

Maria took some of the bundles from Sarah's hands and gladly led her into the house.

"I wished to arrive before the appraisers," Mrs. Hay said. She glanced over her shoulder as footsteps were heard on the front porch and smugly nodded. "I see that I did."

Mr. Purdie, tall and thin, with a solemn manner, entered the house first. Mrs. Hay gave her brother-in-law a stern look. "If you have any doubts about an item's value, I shall be glad to advise you," she said.

"Thank you, madam," Mr. Purdie answered. He formally greeted Clementina, as did the other appraisers: short and chubby Mr. Dixon and kindly Mr. Robert Prentis. To Maria's surprise, Cousin John hurried into the hall, nervously buttoning his coat askew.

"I was appointed to help conduct this inventory because I am familiar with the equipment in the pressroom and all the household items," he explained.

Maria could see that Cousin John was trying hard to be as businesslike as the other men, but he couldn't keep the misery from his face.

Maria watched and listened as her mother greeted the men politely, answered their questions, and began to direct them to the various rooms. But she gasped when Mr. Dixon opened the door to the printing office. "No!" she cried.

Clementina took a quick step forward. "Sir," she

said to Mr. Dixon, "I have been informed by my advisers that the court may allow me to keep my printing equipment."

"I hope that is the case, madam," Mr. Dixon told her. "However, we are duty bound to place a value on every item, whether it is to be sold at this time or not."

Maria found it hard to believe that Mr. Purdie and Mr. Dixon, editors of the other *Gazette*, her father's rivals, and now her mother's, could be in their home, appraising their hard-earned possessions to find out if her father's debts could be paid.

Little Jemmy, tears in his eyes, walked down the stairs and across the hall, coming to a stop in front of Mr. Purdie. Jemmy held out his top, tears welling in his eyes.

"What's this?" Mr. Purdie asked in mock surprise. He waited for Jemmy to answer, but when it was obvious that Jemmy couldn't, Mr. Purdie solemnly shook his head. "A boy's top has no value to an appraiser," he said. "You may keep it."

In surprise, Jemmy blinked back his tears. "Thank you, sir," he said, and hugged his top tightly. He froze, as though having a sudden thought, and asked, "Can Charlie keep his whirligig?"

"Of course," Mr. Purdie answered.

Charlie, who had hung back to watch Jemmy hand

over his top, wailed, "I can't find my whirligig. I've looked all over for it."

Johnny nudged him. "I know where it is," he said.

Charlie looked at him suspiciously. "You hid it, didn't you?"

"Never mind," Johnny answered. "He said you could keep it, so let's find it."

Mr. Purdie turned to Clementina with a wry smile and remarked, "Your lad wouldn't be the first to hide something before an inventory is made. Many find the temptation strong."

Mrs. Hay put an arm around Clementina's shoulders as she scolded her brother-in-law. "We will have no talk of deceit in this house, Alexander."

Flustered, he answered, "I did not mean . . . that is, I was simply telling . . ." He stopped and made a short bow to Clementina. "My apologies, madam, if my careless words have caused you any discomfort."

Clementina answered, "You have caused no discomfort, sir, and your apology is gratefully accepted."

Maria and Sarah walked into the dining room, where Mr. Prentis busily removed items from the drawers of the bowfat chest in one corner.

He took out the silver spoons, examined them, and wrote something on a sheet of paper. As he placed them on the table with the things he had already valued, Maria's resolve to be brave suddenly vanished, and she sat down hard on one of the dining chairs that was lined up against the wall.

"Those were my grandmother's spoons," she whispered to Sarah. "One day they were going to be mine."

"I'm sorry," Sarah said. She held tightly to Maria's hand.

"My father was a good editor and a good printer. It is not his fault he was in debt," Maria said.

Sarah nodded. "It must be terribly hard to have to think about giving up your very own bed and pillow—even your dishes and kitchen pans."

"Our house could be almost empty," Maria said.

Sarah hugged Maria. "It won't be the same as having all your own things, but your house won't be empty." She looked as though she knew a secret she'd promised not to tell. "I wish you never had to think about this, but just wait and see."

It was hard for Maria to be hopeful as she thought about the sale, ten days off. The familiar contents of the house would be on display for all to see and bid on.

"Come now," said Sarah. "Let's do something fun while we have some time to ourselves. Why don't we look at the acrostic in this week's issue of your mother's newspaper?" she asked, pointing to the *Virginia Gazette* on the dining room table.

"I can't," Maria blurted out. "Well, that is, I can't

do it right now. I should probably be helping my mother."

"But there is nothing you can do for her just now. Besides, this newspaper is the only thing the appraisers will not need to inventory. It will be fun. I'll read the first line and you read the second."

Sarah read the first line of the acrostic and waited for Maria to read the next, but the only sound from Maria was a sniffle. When Sarah looked up from the newspaper, she found her friend in tears.

"What is wrong?" Sarah asked anxiously.

Maria blushed, staring down at her toes. "Sarah, I do not read well," she admitted. "I try, but it's difficult." Her voice was little more than a whisper as she added, "I have kept this secret from everyone, except my family. Even you, my dearest friend."

Her eyes wide with surprise, Sarah picked up the newspaper and held it out to Maria. "Here, read the first line of that article," she said.

Maria took a deep breath. Staring hard at the words, she read, "At a . . . a . . . time when—"

"Stop!" Sarah ordered. "Maria, your face is twisted like a wrung-out rag. Is it your eyesight? Can you not see the words?"

"I can see them well," Maria answered.

"Then why are you frowning?"

Maria sighed. "I am trying hard."

Sarah thought a moment. Then she said, "Perhaps you are trying too hard. It looks as if you are pushing the words away, not allowing them to enter your head."

Puzzled, Maria asked, "What do you mean when you say enter my head?"

"Your head must have an open door," Sarah answered. "Look at those little words you struggled with. *At, a, time* . . . You know those words well. Let them in. Then relax with the big words, and they will help you learn what they are."

"How do I do that?"

"Sit comfortably. No, not like that. Do not stiffen your backbone. Relax your shoulders. Stop gripping the newspaper so tightly."

Sarah gave instructions until she was satisfied with Maria's posture. "Now, breathe in and out a few times. Then look at the words. And do not frown!"

Maria did as she was told, then began to read. Sarah was right. The little words were old and familiar. They bounced into her mind. The longer words suddenly did not seem as difficult. She read, "This is the time in which our l-loyalty to our c-colony . . ."

She stopped, rubbing away the tears that blurred her vision. "Oh, Sarah," she cried. She leapt from her chair, dropping the newspaper, and hugged her friend. "Maybe you're right! You already have made reading less frightening for me."

Sarah grinned. "My mother tells me I am a good teacher. I have begun to help our Betsy and Nancy with their letters."

For the first time, Maria dared to hope that soon she would be able to read as well as William. And if she could read as well as William, wouldn't it then be possible to help with the printing of the newspaper? Perhaps even to write a short item for it?

For just an instant, she closed her eyes and pictured a short article that would please all parties and aid her mother's chances of winning the government printing contract.

Maria trembled at the thought of what she might be able to do. Would she dare?

After Sarah and her mother had left, Jemmy and Charlie ran through the cluttered dining room. Maria didn't try to stop them. She joined her mother, who was seated at her desk.

Clementina studied the inventory she had been given and sadly shook her head.

"Our entire household is worth only a little over two hundred and seventy-two pounds," she said. "Dick is valued at thirty pounds because he is strong and healthy. I hope we will be allowed to keep him, because we need his help with the printing presses."

She sighed. "The two letter presses, types, frames, cases for storing the type, and our assorted printing tools were valued at more than our household goods."

"But didn't you say we will be able to keep them, Mama?" Maria reminded her.

"Only until the end of your father's government contract in May."

"What if we win a new government contract?"

"Then I'm sure we can continue to use them."

"We *must* win the contract, Mama," Maria said. She wrapped her arms around her mother, trying to be comforting. What she wished for the most was to be comforted herself.

Chapter Six

During the next few weeks, Maria carried a book wherever she went. At every spare moment she practiced reading the way Sarah had taught her, and she found, to her delight, that her reading *was* improving. But even this triumph was overshadowed by the more somber events in the Rind household.

On a Sunday in early October, the day after the dreaded auction, Maria awoke early. She dressed quickly, aware that no one else was up and about, not even Dick, whose job it was to light fires in the large fireplaces in the hall and kitchen building.

Slowly Maria walked down the stairs and into the hall, with its bare walls and floors. She leaned against the doorframe, remembering, with a pang of sorrow, where a favorite chair or small table had once stood. Now the empty room seemed hollow and cold.

Brushing a tear from her cheek, Maria thought about the crowd of people who had filled the house during the auction. On some pieces there had been spirited bidding. Maria could still see the look of triumph on the face of the woman who had won her mother's china pitcher with the painted roses.

It was the loss of her mother's silver spoons that hurt Maria most. She had left the room when bidding began on the spoons. She didn't want to know who would carry them away.

What's done is done, Maria told herself. There were chores, and there was no time for self-pity. Everyone would be stirring soon. She had breakfast to make—a cold one, since they had only one pot—and later there would be church services to attend.

It was not until late afternoon that someone suddenly knocked loudly at the Rinds' door. Maria was standing closest to the door, so she opened it, then jumped back a step in surprise.

Into the house came Mrs. Hay and her children, Mr. and Mrs. Purdie, the Geddys, the Pelhams, and other neighbors and friends. They carried bedding, a table, assorted straight-backed chairs, kitchen pans and utensils, dishes and cups, and candles in sturdy holders. Sarah giggled and pointed at two of the

Pelham daughters, who carried baskets almost as big as they were.

So this was Sarah's secret! The house was soon filled with people, and the table was covered with food. Maria's eyes burned with tears again, but these were tears of happiness. How good it was to have friends!

When the crowd had gone, Maria surveyed the rooms. They contained less furniture than before, but the Rinds now had most of the things they needed. Maria did not mourn the loss of some of the family's old, familiar possessions. She realized that someday the things their neighbors had brought would become old and familiar. Thankfully, their mother had been able to buy back the printing equipment and some of their possessions, even if it was on credit. Charlie now had his bed, just as Maria had so rashly promised, but she recognized that their household possessions were not really important— not even the precious silver spoons. She shook her head, quickly pushing her thoughts away from the spoons. Only the printing equipment was important, because her mother would make use of it to support the family.

And I will help her, Maria assured herself.

That evening, Maria was stunned by a surprise gift. A young household slave delivered a letter and a small package addressed to Maria.

Maria thanked her, then quickly ran to the bedchamber she shared with her mother to open the package in secret. Who had written the letter? Who had sent her a package? What in the world could be inside it? She had never received a package or a letter before, and her heart beat faster with excitement.

She sat on the small chair and opened the letter, which was written in a clear, round hand. She took a deep breath and began to read it slowly and carefully. She stumbled over some of the words, but her reading was already much improved.

Dear Maria, the letter began, *You are my niece Sarah's dearest friend.*

"Mrs. Purdie!" Maria exclaimed aloud, then continued reading.

Sarah confided in me that she grieved because your mother could not pass on to you her own mother's silver spoons. Sarah is like a daughter to me, because I have no daughters of my own, so it is my great pleasure to grant Sarah's wish that your spoons be returned to your family. Please accept them with my warmest regards and Sarah's love.

Yours in friendship,
Peachy Purdie

Her fingers trembling, Maria finally managed to untie the string and unfold the paper that was wrapped around its contents. As the package lay open on her lap, Maria stared down at the four gleaming silver spoons. What a dear friend she had in Sarah! And how kind Mrs. Purdie had been! Their gift made the spoons seem even more valuable.

Maria carefully wrapped the spoons and carried them downstairs. She gave them, with the letter, to her mother.

Clementina read the letter, then smiled and said, "I will put pen to paper immediately to thank both Mistress Purdie and Sarah."

"Mama," Maria said, "I am the one who should write the letters. Mrs. Purdie's letter and the package were addressed to me."

With a look of surprise, Clementina said, "Perhaps, with some help, you could—"

Maria interrupted. "Mama, I can do it. I would like to try."

"Very well," Clementina said. "I'll bring ink, a quill, and paper from the printing office."

As soon as the supplies were placed in front of her, Maria pulled her chair close to the table and bent over the paper. Since she formed the letters of each word slowly, the ink did not flow smoothly from the quill pen, and tiny blotches dotted the words. Here and there a word looked so messy that she crossed it out and began again.

William suddenly leaned over Maria's shoulder, startling her so that she dropped the quill, shaking a large ink blot onto the paper.

"See what you caused me to do!" she cried.

"One more blot doesn't matter," William said. "Your paper is already quite messy."

"I did my best."

"And you have misspelled *thankful* and *glad*. There is only one *l* in *thankful* and only one *d* in *glad*."

Maria pressed her hands over her eyes. "I must write the letters myself," she said. "I cannot allow Mama to write them for me."

William pulled up a chair and sat next to Maria. "I'll write them for you," he said. "No one will be the wiser."

As Maria hesitated, thinking over his offer, William thumped a finger on her letter and added, "You cannot send a good woman like Mrs. Purdie a letter as messy as this."

"You will really do this for me?" Maria asked.

Grinning, William said, "I will, if you will shine my shoes and brush my clothes every day for one week."

Maria nodded.

"Per note. Two notes, two weeks."

"Two weeks? Very well," Maria said. But as William picked up the quill pen, cleaning it with a soft pen wiper, she quickly said, "But you must write only what I will tell you, and I must sign the letters myself."

"Fair enough," William said. He chose a clean sheet of paper and picked up the pen.

Maria repeated aloud the words she had tried to write and watched William smoothly and skillfully put them on paper. Why were writing and reading so easy for William and so hard for her? Her face burning with embarrassment, Maria carefully signed both letters, trying to make her letters look like William's.

When the ink had dried, she folded each sheet of paper in thirds. William wrote Mrs. Purdie's name on the note addressed to her, and Sarah's name on the other. Then he brought a stub of sealing wax and a candle from the printing office and showed Maria how to seal the letters.

"I'll give them to Dick to deliver," William said. He picked up the letters and was off, running.

Maria sighed. Sarah knew that Maria had trouble

65

reading. Would she notice the neatness of the writing in the letter and guess that Maria had not written it herself? She had not meant to deceive Sarah, but there was no doubt she had. But Sarah had already proved to be a good friend and had helped Maria with her reading. Maria hoped Sarah would be understanding in this matter as well.

Well, what's done is done, Maria thought. There was nothing she could do about it.

But there was something she could do about her penmanship, she decided. With no one to look over her shoulder, she tried again and again to write as neatly and easily as William had. Two or three words were fairly neat—much more so than her first attempts—but still her paper looked a mess.

There was no use wishing that her mother had the time to teach her more about reading and writing. Because of their circumstances it was not possible, so she would continue to try to teach herself.

During the next few weeks, Clementina faithfully published the *Virginia Gazette* every Thursday. And almost every Thursday, Cousin John had a caustic comment to make about William's lack of industry.

"The lad has no interest in becoming a printer," he grumbled.

"Cousin John, William is learning the trade quickly, but he is young and full of boyish spirits,"

Clementina explained. "You cannot expect him to tend to business every waking moment."

On another Thursday, Maria overheard Cousin John remark, "William cannot seem to stick to any job he is given."

"Our situation is difficult, cousin," Clementina answered. "William is doing his best. We are all doing our best. Our subscriptions for the *Gazette* are up. We have received many good comments about the poems and the acrostics we've printed."

Cousin John shook his head. "That is so, but on the other hand, your articles reminding people about the taxes on tea are causing—"

"Dear cousin," Clementina interrupted. "We have always given space to the colonists' point of view."

"The *Gazette*'s motto is 'Open to ALL PARTIES but influenced by NONE.'" Cousin John frowned as he added, "Are you becoming more partisan to grievances against the Crown? It may drive some of our readers away."

Clementina smiled. "Perhaps that is to the good."

"Only if—"

Laughing, she asked, "How did we find ourselves discussing events still on the horizon? What were we speaking of before?"

"Of William," Cousin John answered.

"Let the boy be," Clementina said softly. "He is a

good lad, but he is very young, and the jobs he has been given are taxing."

Cousin John's voice faded as he walked toward the back of the house. "I only wish him to help you more, Clementina."

Maria hadn't meant to overhear the conversation, but now that she had, she couldn't stop thinking about what Cousin John had said. Perhaps she could speak to William and help him realize how much their mother needed his help. But there was nothing she could do about the articles her mother chose to print in her newspaper. Surely it was not good to create enemies. What if people dropped their newspaper subscriptions or stopped buying the *Gazette* altogether? But Maria knew her mother must be true to what she believed. Maria rubbed her forehead. Her head was beginning to hurt.

Later that day, William came into the hall, where Maria was mending a ripped sleeve in Charlie's shirt. "I have some socks you can mend," he told her.

Maria looked up. Her mother was out in the kitchen, Cousin John and Isaac were in the printing office, and the little boys were outside playing with Jemmy's top. "Pray sit with me, William," Maria said. "I wish to talk with you."

A look of curiosity on his face, William sat in the empty chair next to her. "About what?" he asked.

Maria put down her needle and leaned forward. "Every week I have heard Cousin John complain to Mama that you do not help her enough."

William made a face. "Of course I help Mama. You know that."

"I know what I've heard. Cousin John has said that you don't finish jobs you have started."

"Only a few. Some jobs are tedious."

"And that you have no interest in learning the craft of printing."

William grinned at Maria. "I'm a fine apprentice. I'll even be better than Isaac one day soon. I'll like being a printer. Cousin John is behaving like an old grump." William puckered his face and pranced around the hall until Maria could no longer resist and broke into laughter.

"Stop that, William!" she managed to say. "You are impossible!"

"Yes, I am," William said. He ran to the front door, opened it, and said, "Tell Mama I have gone for a game of hoops with John Pelham." The door slammed behind him.

I tried, Maria thought as she picked up Charlie's shirt and returned to her mending. There was nothing else she could do to impress upon Will how much their mother needed his help. If only their mother would realize that in the printing office

Maria would be a much better help than William. No matter how difficult it was to learn to read, she was practicing as often as she could. When her mother needed her, she would be ready.

The family's situation was difficult, but Maria reminded herself, her mother had plans to improve it. As to Cousin John's concern about readers who were disturbed by some of the material her mother put in the *Gazette,* perhaps he was being an old grump in this case, too. He was . . . wasn't he?

For the moment Maria put her concerns aside, refusing to give in to worry.

Chapter Seven

Maria *did* worry, however, when, in Mr. Greenhow's store, she overheard a lively discussion about the daring *Cato's Letters,* which her mother had been publishing.

Although the morning was bright with sun, the chill of the November wind forced Maria to wrap her cloak tightly around her, her head tucked inside the hood like a turtle's in its shell.

A woman who stood with her back to Maria was speaking as Maria entered the store. "I'm afraid Mistress Rind will anger Lord Dunmore and make the situation more difficult," the woman said. "Can you believe she would publish Cato's arguments for liberty? And freedom of expression? My husband says the thoughts expressed in the letters are close to treason."

Maria, her stomach twisted with fear, stepped to one side behind a stack of willow baskets and tried to make herself invisible. *Treason? Mama would publicize treason? How could anyone believe such a thing?*

Someone asked, "Who is this Cato who has written the letters? Is he a Virginia colonist?"

In a shocked tone, the first woman answered, "No, and *Cato* is not the writer's real name. He hid behind this pseudonym when the letters were first published in the London journals."

Another voice spoke up. " 'Tis not only *Cato's Letters* that are causing concern. In my opinion, Clementina Rind was far too bold when she reprinted a letter urging the burgesses to resist the British Parliament's attempts to tax the colonies. Did you not read it?"

"Indeed I did," the first woman said smugly. "The article was based on Cato's idea of representative government. Mrs. Miller pointed this out at tea only yesterday."

Mrs. Miller! Maria shivered. Was the woman set on causing trouble for her mother?

Maria longed to be outside, away from these women, but she had a chore to finish. No matter how frightened she was at having to face them, she was determined not to neglect the duties her mother had given her. Throwing back the hood of her cloak, she walked to the counter, where Mr. Greenhow was carefully folding a length of creamy wool fabric.

From the corner of her eye, Maria saw one of the women nudge the others. They stopped speaking, and each pretended to be busy examining merchandise.

With trembling hands Maria clung to the counter. "Good day, Mr. Greenhow," she said as the shop owner turned toward her with a smile. "Today I need only a packet of darning needles."

Except for Mr. Greenhow's cheery greeting, the room remained silent, but as Maria tucked her package into her pocket and left the store, she could hear a rising buzz of voices behind her.

Maria was eager to tell her mother what she had heard. Her mother must know what people were saying about the newspaper articles she was printing.

Maria found her mother writing at a small desk in the printing office. In one corner of the room, Dick sat at a sewing frame, sewing printed pages to cords. Maria greeted Dick, then quickly glanced at his worktable to see if he would be using any of the beautiful marbled endpapers that came from England.

Dick smiled and shook his head, as if he knew exactly what Maria was hoping to see. "None of those fancy endpapers for these books," he said. "They just some little religious pamphlets."

Maria didn't stop to watch Dick work. Sewing linen thread back and forth across the thick flax cords wasn't the least bit interesting. It was the work with the printing press that was exciting.

When her father had been alive and well, Dick had worked as beater, using ink balls to spread a mixture of varnish and lampblack evenly on the type, which had been set and locked into metal frames. It was her father, working as puller, who cranked the carriage of the huge wooden press into place, then pulled hard on the bar attached to the screw that pressed the paper against the inky type.

Over and over again, the two of them had worked in rhythm, printing one sheet of paper at a time. It was hard work, and during the warmest months their shirts were soaked with sweat. But Maria remembered that when the job was finished and the newspaper was ready to be distributed, her father's face glowed with satisfaction. To her surprise, Maria realized that lately she had seen the same look on her mother's face when she had finished each issue's print run.

Oh, Papa, Maria thought in anguish, *why did you have to leave us?*

Maria knew that she had no time to mourn her father now. She was wasting time. It was important to speak to her mother about what she had heard.

As Maria began to walk past him, Dick said, "Don't you go botherin' your mother now. She's busy writin' somethin' for her *Gazette*."

Clementina raised her head and held out one arm to Maria. "I have time for you, daughter. I've been staring at what I have written, wondering how to say what I want to say in the best way possible." She smiled. "That's part of writing, trying to make sense of your thoughts, and sometimes changing completely what you have already written."

Maria accepted her mother's hug. Still leaning against her, she took a long breath and quickly said, "Mama, we may have problems with what you choose to put in your *Gazette*."

As her mother looked up, surprised, Maria told her about the conversation she had overheard.

When she had finished, Clementina said, " 'Tis no matter what people might say. I must be true to what I believe."

"But if people are upset by your articles, they may not buy the newspaper."

Clementina smiled. "Our subscriptions have risen each week. Whether they agree with me or not, people do want to read what I print."

She got up from her desk and opened a wooden box. "Here are current letters from our subscribers," she said. "Some of them tell me how much they enjoy a newspaper written with a woman's viewpoint. And many have written to thank me for printing in the *Gazette* the letters I receive complaining about British imperial policies."

Surprised, Maria asked, "Do none of the letters criticize, as did the women in Mr. Greenhow's store?"

Clementina sat down, taking Maria's hands in her own. "There will always be those who criticize, daughter. But our *Gazette* must include the views of colonists who feel British policy tramples on our rights as subjects of the Crown."

"What about those colonists who think British policies are proper?" Maria asked. "Does not the *Gazette* represent them, too?"

Laughing, Clementina said, "My dear, practical Maria. Yes, our newspaper is for all readers. And remember, we are all good subjects of the Crown; our grievances don't make us disloyal."

" 'Open to ALL PARTIES but influenced by NONE,' " Maria quoted. "Your motto."

For a moment Clementina was silent. Finally she said, "No matter how much opposition I have, I refuse to give up my belief that people should be represented and governed fairly."

"Then you will be fair, too, Mama," Maria said.

Clementina's voice dropped, as if she were talking to herself. "In the packet from the last ship to arrive from England was a magazine article justifying Britain's need to tax the colonies in order to pay for their defense. Not all taxation is wrong—only taxation without representation. So a defense tax is understandable. I could reprint this article without compromising my views." She looked into Maria's eyes. "Is this what you mean by being fair?"

Maria hugged her mother. "If you are too critical of the Crown, I am so afraid you will not only lose your readers, but you will not be chosen to be government printer when the burgesses meet in May. If you do not win the contract we will lose our printing equipment and our furniture. Don't forget you have only a few months' credit to pay for them." She shivered.

Clementina held Maria tightly. "Do not be afraid, daughter. I have a practical nature, too. It was a group of burgesses who brought us to Williamsburg—to print a different point of view. They and their friends will not desert us now. Your father would be proud of how I am continuing to care for our family. I will not disappoint him. I will not disappoint you."

Maria could feel her mother's heart beat a little

faster as she added, "But I am a Virginian as well as a British subject, and I cannot change that."

After the exchange she had overheard in Mr. Greenhow's store, Maria knew just how important it was for her to become a good reader, so that she could see for herself what her mother was publishing in the *Gazette*. Although her reading had improved greatly, she'd never been able to get through a whole issue of the newspaper. She was determined to do it.

In the weeks following her mother's publication of *Cato's Letters*, Maria faithfully practiced reading whenever she could snatch a few moments. One day, she determined to finish the most recent issue of the *Gazette*. She carried it with her while she did her chores and read as much as she could while the boys were doing theirs. Forcing herself, straining to sound out each word, she struggled painfully through every word, sentence, and line. It took longer than she would have liked, but she read all four pages. When she was finished, she clutched the paper to herself and smiled in triumph. Her mother would be so proud!

Maria couldn't wait to tell her when she came out of the printing room. Now she could help her mother with both the housework and the newspaper. But with the ability to read came the discovery that what her mother was publishing in the *Gazette* was dangerous. And that led to even more worries.

True to her word, her mother had reprinted the article from the British magazine justifying Britain's need to tax the colonies to pay for defense. But she had continued to make certain her readers knew that Parliament had not removed the import tax on tea. In the December sixteenth issue of the *Gazette,* she actually warned women that "tea kept too long will breed an insect which would render the drink pernicious to the health."

Maria gave up trying to puzzle out what the word *pernicious* meant, but she was sure it must be something dreadful. Her mother ended the article with a warning to be very careful when buying tea, especially tea imported from London. "The surest way to be safe," she wrote, "is to drink none."

Letting the newspaper drop to her lap, Maria sadly shook her head. Surely this time her mother had gone too far.

The printing office was always busy. There was the weekly newspaper to get out, and the regular government printing, and also the annual almanac. On top of that, there were pamphlets and essays to be printed for sale in the printing office or for customers who had ordered them. The members of the Rind family had little time to spare.

One night, after Johnny, Charlie, and Jemmy had been tucked into bed, Maria entered the pressroom, where her mother, Cousin John, William, and Dick were still hard at work.

As she saw the exhaustion on their faces, she said, "Let me help."

"Maria can do my job!" offered William, who was working as beater.

"No!" Clementina answered sharply. She sighed and spoke quietly. "William, you have been taught how to be a beater. Maria has not."

Dick pulled the bar that turned the screw, pressing the platen on the tipen, with its sheet of paper, against the type. When he lifted it, he paused and said, "There is a job that Maria can do. She can sort the type."

Clementina hesitated. "I'm not sure she knows her letters well enough."

"I do, Mama," Maria said quickly. "I try to find time each day to work at my lessons."

Clementina smiled at Maria, unable to hide her expression of surprise. "That greatly pleases me," she said, but she looked hesitant as Cousin John took Dick's place at the press and Dick led Maria over to one of the typecases.

The typecases were on frames that were tables with tall legs. Covering the tops of the cases were small, open boxes, some of them containing narrow pieces of lead with a raised letter on one edge. Resting at an angle above the top of the cases were a series of matching open boxes.

Dick handed Maria a large ink-stained container filled with a jumble of the squares of lead type. "You have to go through these, one by one," he said, "then put them into the boxes they belong in on the case. Capital letters go into the upper case. The little letters go into the lower case. Can you do that?"

"Yes," Maria answered, although she wasn't sure she could.

As Dick took over the job Cousin John had been doing—hanging each printed sheet of paper to dry—Maria picked up one of the small pieces of type. It was about an inch high and narrow. On one end was a letter—capital *M*. She reached toward the upper case, counted the squares from left to right, and decided where the *M* should be. She dropped it into the small box and reached for another letter.

Sorting the type seemed to take forever. She was still not through when the printing stopped.

Maria's mother stepped up beside her. "You've almost finished, but I will help," she said. Her fingers flew over the pieces of type, dropping each letter quickly into its proper place.

The container was almost empty, and Maria smiled with relief. This was a tedious job, and she was happy they had finished it. But suddenly Cousin John brought over the forme that held the lines of type that had been fastened in the press.

As Maria looked at all the many lines of type with dismay, she heard her mother say, "It's late. Sorting this type can wait until morning."

William rubbed an ink-stained hand across his forehead, brushing his hair from his eyes. "How do you like the printing business now?" he teased Maria.

Maria stubbornly lifted her chin. "Sorting type is not as difficult as roasting a chicken and peeling potatoes. Besides, I like working with Mama."

She walked close to Clementina as they left the printing office, pleased when her mother rested an arm across her shoulders as they began to climb the stairs.

"Did you hear the boys' prayers before they went to bed?" Clementina asked Maria.

"Yes, Mama. When you are not there at bedtime, I always listen to their prayers."

A note of sorrow crept into Clementina's voice. "Oh, how I wish I could hear their prayers myself, but we have been so very busy. There are printing jobs that must be done."

"I know, Mama," Maria said. "It's all right. The boys are excited by the news that a traveler reported a light cover of snow just north of town. They are sure we'll have snow right here in Williamsburg by Christmas day."

Clementina suddenly stopped and made a strange sound, almost like a sob.

Maria looked up quickly. "Mama?" she asked in surprise. "What is the matter?"

Her mother sat on the stairs, and Maria quickly dropped to sit beside her.

"We have been fortunate to keep our printing equipment and to gain new subscribers and new orders for other work," Clementina explained, "but we are still in debt. I doubt even our Christmas day dinner will be anything out of the ordinary."

"Oh, Mama, that doesn't matter. All that is important is that we are together," Maria said.

"The boys will be disappointed."

"Perhaps at first," Maria said, "but I will explain to them why they can't always have what they wish for."

With her elbows on her knees, Clementina rested her head in her hands. "I wish that I could afford to make a feast as when your father was alive. That at least might comfort us now that he is gone," she said.

Maria snuggled against her mother. "We have each other. We have a home. We have love. We can remember Papa. That is enough, Mama."

Clementina put an arm around Maria, pulling her close. For a long time they sat quietly, not speaking.

But Maria's mind was racing. She felt the way she had when she was small and a storm swept up from the ocean, howling and rattling doors and windows as it spread across the land. No matter how fearful, no matter what the damage to roofs and trees, the storms had always passed. This storm that darkened the lives of her family was bound to leave. If Mama did not anger too many people, if she could win a contract again with the burgesses and be appointed government printer . . .

Maria sighed. With all her heart she believed the storm would pass, but she wished there was something she could do to make it pass quickly.

She climbed to her feet and held out a hand to her mother. "Mama," Maria said. "It is very late. Let's go to bed."

Chapter Eight

The narrow winter sunbeams that streamed through the windows of Bruton Parish Church on Christmas day were as clear and brittle as the thin ice that covered the edges of the pond. They lightly touched some of the sprigs of pine and holly that decorated the church, releasing a tangy, woodsy scent. Maria leaned against the back of the pew and closed her eyes, breathing in the fragrance of Christmas. She was pleased to be in church with her mother and Cousin John.

Her younger brothers were at home under Dick's watchful eye, but William and Isaac sat patiently, which was unlike William's usual behavior. Their hair was combed, their clothes tidy.

Maria had explained to her brothers that they

must be practical, that there was scant money this year for a large feast or extra treats of candy or cake. But they hadn't wanted to accept what she had said.

As Jemmy had pouted, Maria had asked, "Whose birthday do we celebrate on Christmas?"

Jemmy had had to think a minute. Then his eyes had widened with excitement. "Mine?" he asked.

"No," she'd answered. "It's the birthday of Jesus."

His lower lip had curled again. "When is it *my* birthday?" he'd demanded.

Maria had scooped him up in a hug. "In the spring," she'd told him. "And for your birthday I will make a special pudding—just for you."

Her offer hadn't satisfied him. But Jemmy was only three, Maria reminded herself. How could he really understand?

Reverend John Bracken, rector of the church, began his sermon, and Maria tried to keep her mind on his words. But it was too difficult. She was thankful for the fat goose her mother had been given in payment for a small printing job. She and her mother had dressed and cleaned and salted the goose, and now it was roasting on a spit over the fire, with Dick to watch and turn it.

To accompany the goose Maria had made a special cranberry-orange relish. She also had prepared winter vegetables—turnips, carrots, and potatoes—and had sliced more than a dozen dried apples, stewing them until the water, sugar, and cinnamon she'd added had formed a thick syrup. They would have a meal smaller than their usual Christmas fare this afternoon, but the boys would no longer tease her about her cooking. Maria was proud of herself for learning to cook well enough to please her family.

Suddenly remembering she was in church on a very holy day, Maria said a silent prayer that all would go well with her family during the coming year. Perhaps it was not fair to Mr. Purdie and Mr. Dixon to ask God's help in awarding the government printing contract to her mother, but Maria made the request anyway. With the inflammatory articles her mother persisted in reprinting and writing, she needed all the help that could be given.

Mr. Purdie and Mr. Dixon had recently printed an anonymous letter in their *Gazette* from someone claiming to be a friend to Mrs. Rind but accusing her of bias in not publishing an article he had sent to her. It was an article highly critical of a citizen of Williamsburg.

Maria remembered that her mother had shaken her head when she had received the article. "My newspaper will not be used to harm someone's reputation," she said. "It would be better if the writer took his complaints to a court of law."

Maria was curious. "What does the writer say, Mama?" she had asked.

" 'Tis of no matter," Clementina had answered, tossing the pages of the rival *Gazette* into a box at the side of her desk. "I will not change my mind about printing this piece—especially because the writer does not have the courage to sign the article with his name."

But she would not let the matter drop, because the anonymous writer accused her of not following her own pledge to maintain a spirit of freedom in her newspaper. Maria was worried, even though her mother was not. The controversy could make their situation even worse. No matter that her mother had told her not to worry. Maria could clearly see that without a government contract and its guaranteed income, their printing equipment would have to be sold to help pay her father's debts. No printing equipment, no printing office, no house, no way that her mother could support her children.

Maria had read the piece Clementina had written in answer to the anonymous writer. It was to be set in type and printed on December thirtieth in her newspaper. She insisted that in spite of the severe reprimand by "An Attentive Observer," as he signed himself, she would not print the article in question until the anonymous author made public his name. Maria had memorized the last line of her mother's written answer: "I am not conscious of having deviated from the spirit of freedom, which I shall always think it my duty to maintain."

For a moment Maria clenched her hands together and squeezed her eyes shut. *Mama has a duty to support her family, too. She must win that government contract. She must!*

"Amen!" Reverend Bracken said loudly.

Maria jumped, then silently echoed, "Amen!"

The Christmas dinner that afternoon was every bit as good as Maria had hoped it would be. And later, friends came by to wish them good cheer.

Mrs. Hay, accompanied by her five children, arrived with a basket. "This was resting at your doorstep," Mrs. Hay said as she handed it to Clementina.

All the children gathered around, Charlie and Jemmy pushing to be first to see what was in the basket.

William reached over their heads to pull out a paper twist of sugar candy. "There are apples and nuts, too!" he cried.

Maria saw her mother's puzzled look as she asked Mrs. Hay, "Is this from you?"

Mrs. Hay shook her head. "Truly, it is not. Is there nothing to identify the sender?"

"I will look," Maria told her.

"I'll help you," Sarah said. She giggled. "I love solving puzzles."

Maria handed each of her little brothers a piece of the candy to keep them busy. When they had run off to share with the Hay children, she thoroughly examined the basket. The polished red apples gleamed like jewels. Even the deep golden shells of the hickory nuts shone like pebbles in a brook. Tucked into the middle of the basket was a jar of quince marmalade, its top sealed with mutton fat.

"Look!" Sarah cried as she pointed to a card half hidden behind an apple. "There's a note! Oh, I knew we'd solve the puzzle!"

Maria pulled out the card and read it silently. *For the children* was all it said.

Sarah read it aloud, but she suddenly cried, "Oh!" and clapped a hand over her mouth.

Maria looked at her. "Oh?" she asked. "What does that mean? Do you know whose penmanship this is?"

"I simply said 'Oh,' " Sarah answered, but she quickly glanced at her mother.

"What's all this secrecy?" Mrs. Hay asked. Giggling, she leaned over Clementina's shoulder to read the note as Maria handed it to her mother.

"You can see it is not my hand," Mrs. Hay began. But she suddenly quieted, stepping back.

She recognizes the handwriting, too, Maria thought. *It belongs to someone they both know well. With a jolt, she realized she had seen that clear, rounded hand-writing, too. Mrs. Purdie's.*

Maria was about to ask Sarah if she was right, but she saw with surprise a fleeting look of hurt and sor-row on her mother's face. Jemmy ran with sticky hands and mouth to hug his mother, and the look vanished, replaced by a smile. But Maria guessed that her mother was torn between wanting her children to enjoy the sweets and fruits and not having to de-pend on someone else to give them what their own mother was unable to provide.

Later, as the early dusk descended and candlelight disappeared into the deep shadows in the hall, the Rind children sang hymns for Christmas, led by their mother.

This was the family's first Christmas without their father, and Maria ached with loneliness for him. But she followed the example of her mother, who smiled and directed the singing with enthusiasm, her voice as deep and strong as the church bells. Isaac and William soon joined in, hesitantly at first, and Dick could be heard singing along from the hall.

Clementina read the Christmas story from the Bible, just as their father used to do. Then she an-nounced that it was time they all went to bed. In the morning they would rise early, because there was much work to be done.

Cousin John carried Jemmy upstairs to the boys' bedchamber, and Maria took her candlestick into the bedchamber she shared with her mother. She undressed to her shift and snuggled deep down under the quilt. Soon her own body heat warmed her, but she was unable to sleep. In spite of the family celebration of Christmas day, it was not the same without her father.

Needing her mother, Maria was glad to hear Clementina's footsteps on the stairs and see the door to their room open. She raised her head to greet her mother but was startled to hear muffled sobs.

When Clementina climbed under the quilt, Maria threw her arms around her mother and whispered, "I miss Papa, too."

Clementina reached out, drawing Maria close. Holding each other tightly, they cried together until they finally fell asleep.

In the morning Maria awoke to find that her mother had already dressed and gone downstairs. She could hear muffled voices and footsteps in the hall.

Maria washed her face, dressed, and brushed her hair, tucking it carefully under her cap. Then she hurried down the stairs.

The door to the pressroom stood open, so Maria stepped inside. Her mother was standing by the press, holding up a printed sheet of paper, examining it for flaws.

Clementina, in complete control, smiled at Maria. "Good morning, daughter," she said, then looked back at the printed sheet.

For a moment Maria was puzzled by the change in her mother from the night before, but she realized that to her mother there was nothing that could be said about the tears that had been shed. Maria and Clementina had both given in to their loneliness, their sorrow, their worries, and their fears. But that lapse was over and would not happen again.

"Good morning, Mama," Maria answered. She paused, then added, "Could I help you in the printing office again today?"

Clementina raised one eyebrow, sharing a moment of humor with Maria. "I think you will be of much greater use keeping the boys from trying to eat all the apples and nuts at one time."

As Cousin John entered the office, tying his apron, Clementina said, "Cousin, word has come through the Boston press that the northern ports have refused to allow the landing of a large shipment of tea from England."

Cousin John raised his head, startled. "Refused?"

he asked. "But that would mean resistance to the port authorities. Can they do this?"

"They have done so," Clementina answered firmly. "And so far the British authorities have not taken action. However, no one knows what this will lead to." Her eyes shone as she added, "The news will be the talk of the town."

Maria's stomach knotted with fear. "Mama!" she cried. "You must not praise the colonists for their resistance!"

"Child, do not worry your head about things that do not concern you," Clementina said. "Besides, I am merely reporting the incident." Impatiently, she pointed toward the hallway. "Pray leave and tend to your duties. I have much work to do."

Maria quietly left, shutting the door between the home and the printing office. But as she walked to the hall, where her brothers were playing, she knew she would be unable to obey her mother's order not to worry. What her mother was doing did concern Maria. And since her mother did not worry, Maria would have to worry for both of them.

Chapter Nine

Maria realized that her mother had been right about Williamsburg being abuzz with the news. Wherever she went, she heard people talking about Boston's refusal to allow the tea cargo to be landed. Some of the *Virginia Gazette*'s readers were excited, some were angry, and some seemed fearful.

"This will show Parliament and King George!"

"There is no reason for Clementina Rind to print the details of the meetings of the Sons of Liberty in New York. A group of hotheads, to be sure!"

"They are not hotheads! They are patriots!"

"I beg to differ. The Sons of Liberty are hotheads! Their actions are not deserving of coverage in the *Gazette*. Do you remember how often Mr. Rind supported the boycott of tea in the pages of his *Gazette* in 1770 and 1771?"

"East India Company tea may be inexpensive, but there is still a tax on it!"

"It's Parliament's right to tax citizens of the empire."

"No. We must make our grievances known—and that is what the Bostonians are doing."

"Grievances against whom? The British? *We* are British!"

Maria pushed through crowded Market Square early in the morning after the news first appeared in Thursday's *Gazette*. She wished she could clap her hands over her ears and run from the babble of voices. But then she heard a clear, strong voice say, "Listen to Clementina Rind. Her *Gazette* tells us what we need to know."

Curious, Maria glanced around. She did not know who had spoken; but a man, bent under a heavy sack of potatoes resting on his shoulder, chuckled as he said, "What is printed in her *Gazette* should be of no surprise."

However, on the following Thursday, January 6, 1774, Maria thought of what the man had said and how surprised he would be at what he read that day in the *Gazette*. Her mother reported the astonishing news that had just reached Virginia: Three weeks earlier, on December sixteenth, a large group of men in Boston, dressed like Indians to hide their identities, had boarded the three British ships in the harbor—the *Dartmouth* first, then the *Eleanor,* and last the *Beaver.* They chopped open all the tea chests and dumped the entire cargo of tea into Boston Harbor. No one was harmed, and no other cargo was touched. By nine o'clock at night the raid was over.

People in Williamsburg were shocked and excited. Some were openly fearful of what the British authorities might do to retaliate.

" 'Twas a bold move, to be sure," Maria heard Mr. Greenhow tell a customer in his store. He chuckled as he added, "King George and Parliament will now learn that the colonists' grievances must be taken seriously."

In a scolding voice a woman answered, " 'Twould be far better for the colonists to try to make amends to the Crown before some drastic action is taken."

Maria looked up to see that the customer was Mrs. Miller. She spoke with such force that her hat bobbled on her head like a toy boat on a pond.

Mrs. Hay, who also stood at the counter, answered, "We have tried reasoning with Parliament and King George before. It did little good with the Stamp Act in 1765. It took protest to get that repealed, don't forget. According to Clementina Rind—"

Mrs. Miller interrupted loudly. "You should be reading your brother-in-law's newspaper and not the inflammatory words of Mrs. Rind."

Her cheeks turning red, Mrs. Hay said, "Mrs. Rind's *Gazette* is not inflammatory. She prints the truth."

"It does not matter," Mrs. Miller said. "Her *Virginia Gazette* will soon come to an end." Her lips stretched in a tight smile. "Surely you are aware that Mr. Purdie and Mr. Dixon have made it known that they will apply for the appointment of government printer in May."

Maria gasped. Her mother had said they might, but Maria had pushed this worry out of her mind.

Someone spoke up. "Mr. Purdie considers himself to be as wedded to the truth as Mrs. Rind."

"Maybe so, but they are not of the same mold," Mrs. Miller said. "Mr. Purdie and Mr. Dixon temper their opinions. They do not deliberately antagonize."

Before anyone else had a chance to speak, Mrs. Miller said, " 'Tis rumored that two of our burgesses—I shall not mention their names—have expressed their desire for the position to be given to Mr. Purdie and Mr. Dixon."

Maria didn't wait to purchase what she needed. Jumping from the steps of John Greenhow's store, she raced down Duke of Gloucester Street to her home.

Once inside the house, she leaned against the door frame, trying to catch her breath.

Clementina, who was on her way into the printing office, stopped and looked at Maria in surprise. "What has happened to you, daughter?" she asked.

Maria managed to tell her mother what she had overheard. "Mr. Purdie and Mr. Dixon wish to be the official government printer, instead of you," she said. "They have made it known they are planning to apply."

"It was your father who received the contract, not I," Clementina said calmly, but a wrinkle appeared between her brows, and Maria could see that she had been shaken by the news.

"You are going to apply for the appointment, aren't you?" Maria asked.

"Of course," Clementina told her. "I have always delivered the government printing in a timely and careful manner. The burgesses should be pleased. There is no reason to remove me from the position."

Maria wasn't calmed by her mother's brave words. Instead, she grew even more fearful. "Could you leave out news about the import tax on tea and how brave the people up north were in preventing the East India Company tea from being landed?"

Clementina sighed and took Maria's hands into her own. "Dear daughter," she said, "these are difficult times, but I must continue to stand fast for what I believe. Remember, your father won the contract handily, even though he was invited to Williamsburg to give voice to opposition to British colonial practices."

Maria looked up into her mother's dark eyes. "Is there nothing you can print about the royal government or our governor that will not anger people?"

"My poems and acrostics are very popular."

"I mean news stories, Mama," Maria said.

"But neither the British authorities nor Governor Dunmore have done anything recently that I could praise."

"Perhaps they will." Maria thought a moment. "Papa used to say that a newspaper publisher's job is to keep his eyes and ears open, to discover stories that people want to read."

Clementina smiled and hugged Maria. "Very well," she said. "I will heed your father's good advice, and *if* the authorities do something praiseworthy, I shall include it."

Jemmy suddenly bellowed with rage from a back room, and Clementina stepped aside. "Pray see why Jemmy is so angry with his brothers. I must return to work."

Maria hurried to settle an argument over whose

turn it was to spin the top. But her mind was on the conversation she had just had with her mother. She admired her mother's bravery. She was proud of her for standing up for what she believed. But she was afraid that her mother's devotion to truth might worsen the family's precarious position.

During the next few weeks, articles in the Rinds' *Gazette* continued to discourage readers from drinking tea. A reprinted article from Boston even informed readers that a ship bringing tea to the colonies had plague and smallpox on board. Clementina pointed out that it was reasonable to think that the tea had been tainted by the diseases, so those who drank the tea would be at great risk.

Not a single news story favored the British authorities. Maria sighed and wondered if her mother had given any thought at all to their conversation.

Then, toward the middle of February, during the evening meal, Clementina mentioned to her family that Lady Charlotte Dunmore and her children—all but the youngest—would soon arrive in Williamsburg to join her husband, John Murray, fourth Earl of Dunmore and the Crown-appointed governor of Virginia.

Johnny paused, his spoon halfway to his mouth. "Why can't the youngest come, too?" he asked.

"It is a long, hard sea journey from England to

Virginia," Clementina explained. "The little lad is only about eighteen months old—too young to make the journey in good health."

Maria thought how sad it would be for a woman to have to leave her baby and travel so far from her home, especially to join a husband who was so disagreeable in nature. "Why is Lady Dunmore coming to Virginia?" she asked.

Her mother looked surprised. "Because her husband has requested her to come and make a home for him here. A good wife does her best to please her husband."

"Even if she has to leave her baby?"

"It has been two years since Lord Dunmore left England. I'm sure he has been very lonely for his wife and children."

"Two years? Then he has never seen his baby."

Clementina picked up her spoon, saying, "Maria, your mutton broth is very tasty."

"Thank you, Mama," Maria answered. She was well aware that her mother had just ended the conversation, but there was more Maria wanted to say. "How hard it must be for Lady Dunmore to spend weeks traveling across the sea to a land that must be so different from England."

As her mother looked up, puzzled, Maria continued. "And the children—did they sorrow at leaving their friends behind? Did they wonder if they'd ever see their home in England again?"

Clementina smiled. Then she laughed. "My practical little daughter," she said. "Sometimes you are wiser than the rest of us."

William shook his head. "Not Maria," he said. "She's not wiser than me."

"All of you dear children are wise in your own ways," Clementina said. "Maria has been wise in keeping her eyes and ears open."

William swallowed the last bite of his bread with a gulp. "I don't understand, Mama. What is Maria doing? What are you talking about?"

Clementina winked at Maria. "Wait and see," she said. "You'll soon find out."

Close to seven o'clock in the evening on Saturday, February 26, 1774, Lady Charlotte Dunmore and her six children, accompanied by Dunmore's secretary, arrived in Williamsburg. Maria took her little brothers to Palace Street, where all the houses were bright with candlelight, to watch the carriages pull to a stop at the Governor's Palace. Many of the citizens of Williamsburg had come to show honor to Lady Dunmore, in spite of their dislike for her ill-tempered husband.

There were many long speeches, and the boys squirmed with boredom. But to their joy, there was a cannon salute that caused them to clap their hands over their ears, jump with excitement, and shout.

"Fireworks later!" Charlie shouted at Maria. "The man over there said there would be fireworks!"

"What are fireworks?" Jemmy asked.

Charlie laughed. "You'll find out!" he said.

Maria immediately remembered her mother saying, "You'll find out," in answer to William's question. Since that evening Maria had been pleased that her mother had so quickly understood her idea. The arrival of Lady Dunmore was Clementina's chance to write something pleasing about the governor, Lord Dunmore, who represented the Crown in Virginia.

What would her mother write about this day? Maria was eager to find out.

On March 3, 1774, both *Virginia Gazette*s were published.

Maria quickly snatched up a copy of her mother's newspaper, excited to find not only a long, detailed description of Lady Dunmore's arrival, with the names of her children and governor Dunmore's secretary and his wife, who accompanied the family to Virginia. To Maria's delight, she discovered that her mother had written a poem in praise of Lady Dunmore.

"Hail, noble Charlotte! Welcome to the plain," it began. It was highly complimentary of Lady Dunmore, and it expressed a great joy at her presence in Williamsburg.

Maria struggled to read every word in the article, proud of her mother for writing such a fine tribute. She was positive that it was better than any tribute Mr. Purdie may have printed.

On her trip to Mr. Greenhow's store, Maria saw a copy of Purdie and Dixon's *Gazette*. It took only a minute to find what they had written about Lady Dunmore's arrival.

It was a simple, formal notice of her safe voyage, next to the printed texts of the speeches given by the college faculty, mayor, and aldermen. Two anonymous poems were included, but they were poems that could have served to honor any official.

Maria dropped the newspaper and grinned. Her mother had written a wonderful tribute from one woman to another. Readers who had complained that Clementina Rind's newspaper showed too much bias against the Crown would have nothing to complain about now.

Not even Mrs. Miller.

Chapter Ten

Maria's joy over her mother's tribute to Lady Dunmore did not last long. Sales of that issue of the *Gazette* were brisk, and there were many comments from pleased readers. But in the next few issues Clementina continued to print news stories and letters that leaned toward voicing grievances against Crown policies. She continued to urge readers to give up drinking tea, even printing on the front page a sorrowful poem written to a set of china banished from use because of the import tax on tea. To buy any tea would give silent approval of the tax.

Wherever Maria went, she overheard people discussing the two *Virginia Gazette*s. There were comments favorable to her mother, which Maria repeated to herself over and over because they gave her courage. But many preferred Mr. Purdie's and Mr. Dixon's muted response to Parliament and the Crown, and their remarks frightened Maria.

Soon the House of Burgesses would convene, which meant that her mother would submit her petition, asking for appointment as public printer of the colony.

Maria tried hard to keep her eyes and ears open, searching for any bit of news that would interest her mother yet would still put the British policies in a good light. Her mother had pleased everyone with her tribute to Lady Dunmore. Could there be another favorable story about Lady Dunmore?

Maria questioned her mother that evening, after the family had been fed and the younger boys were asleep in their bedchamber. "Mama," Maria asked, "now that Lady Dunmore has been in Virginia for a few weeks, how does she?"

Clementina looked up from her sewing. "I have no idea. Why do you wish to know?"

Cousin John put down his book and also looked at Maria. Even William idly glanced up from the slate on which he was adding and subtracting.

Blushing, Maria tried to put her thoughts into an idea that would interest her mother. "I mean, does Lady Dunmore enjoy our Virginia spring climate? Are her children happy? Are their tutors continuing the education they began in England? What is their family life like in the Governor's Palace?"

Clementina raised one eyebrow. "I doubt this is idle curiosity on your part, daughter. Are you hoping I will again write something complimentary about Lady Dunmore?"

"Perhaps your readers would be interested," Maria answered.

"And perhaps they would not," Clementina said. "In any case, more important matters need to be published. I do not have the space to include articles about Lady Dunmore and her children."

"But readers were happy when you wrote that tribute to her." Maria quickly added, "Your article and poem were far better than those in Mr. Purdie's and Mr. Dixon's *Gazette*."

"They were indeed," Clementina agreed. "But there is a limit to what I can write concerning our governor's wife."

"If you could but balance your news—"

Clementina went back to her sewing. "I appreciate your concern, daughter, but it is unnecessary."

John surprised Maria by speaking up. "Is it, Cousin? Because Purdie and Dixon are hopeful they will win the printing contract."

"I am just as hopeful," Clementina answered without looking up. She carefully folded her sewing and placed it in her sewing basket.

Cousin John did not give up. " 'Tis true, madam, that if your husband were here, he would openly air grievances against British authority by what he chose to publish. But as a woman you may need to be more careful."

"With all my heart, I wish he were here," Clementina said. She stood, looking down at Cousin John. "But he is not, and I must do what I feel is best. Pray excuse me. William . . . Maria . . . it is late and time to retire."

Maria went to bed with a tightness in her chest that wouldn't go away. She tried to comfort herself by remembering that her open-minded father had won the contract before. And she knew her mother was doing what she thought was right in taking a strong stand. But what if she was wrong?

On the morning of Saturday, May 7, 1774, the House of Burgesses convened. Maria begged her mother to allow her to accompany Cousin John to the Capitol as the petition was presented. "Pray ask William to watch the boys so that I may go with him," she said.

Clementina smiled and replied, "Cousin John is merely going to listen outside the door just to make sure the petition comes up. Why are you so eager to be there, daughter?"

Maria didn't want to tell her mother that for the past few weeks she couldn't sleep for worrying about that contract. She had tried to talk to Cousin John about it, but his forehead had wrinkled and his lips pursed as if he had a bad taste in his mouth.

"I would not be truthful if I told you that I think your mother will be awarded the printing contract," he said.

This was not what Maria had thought he would answer. She had gasped and asked, "Do you think she will not?"

Cousin John had looked away and shrugged. "I have no way of knowing what the burgesses will decide."

As Maria now studied her mother's face, she could see that in spite of her reassuring smile, there was worry in her eyes and her cheeks were pale. "I wish to learn the outcome of the burgesses' decision as soon as possible," Maria said.

Clementina put an arm around Maria's shoulders and answered, "I'm certain that Cousin John will be happy to have your company, daughter."

Maria scrubbed her face and hands, dressed in her neatest cotton gown, and walked at Cousin John's side down Duke of Gloucester Street to the Capitol. By the time they reached the Capitol, Maria's heart was thumping loudly with excitement, and her legs were trembling.

As they approached the imposing Capitol, with its clock tower and tall weather vane, Maria saw Mr. Purdie and Mr. Dixon standing at one side of the east hall, talking with friends.

As Maria and her cousin walked under the portico, just outside the chamber where the House of Burgesses would meet, both Mr. Purdie and Mr. Dixon acknowledged Cousin John with a short, polite bow, then went back to their conversation.

Maria glanced through the open doors into the dark wood-paneled chamber where the House of Burgesses met. She stared in awe at the round windows behind and at each side of the high, impressive Speaker's chair. In a half circle behind the Speaker's chair and along each side of the chamber were green upholstered chairs and benches for the burgesses. In the middle of the chamber was a large table on which were stacks of papers. Many of the burgesses were already present, talking with each other in small groups.

Maria was startled to discover, when Cousin John handed her mother's petition to a clerk, that none of the petitioners would speak before the burgesses.

Her heart began to beat a little more slowly and it was easier to breathe as she stood at the doorway, watching the Speaker, Mr. Peyton Randolph, take his seat and call the session to order.

Now, Maria thought, *they will read our petitions.*

But instead, two new burgesses recited the oath of office and took their places with the others.

Now! Maria thought hopefully, and she pressed her free hand against her stomach, which was beginning to hurt.

But another petition was read to the burgesses by a clerk with a droning voice. The petition had been written by a lighthouse keeper at the fort at Old Point Comfort. To Maria, his detailed description of his careful service to all ships coming in from the sea and passing up and down Chesapeake Bay lasted much too long. She couldn't help fidgeting until the clerk finally read the gentleman's request to be paid an annual stipend judged adequate to his service.

She had expected the burgesses to decide either for or against the lighthouse keeper's petition, but, instead, it was ordered that the petition be referred to the consideration of the Committee of Trade, which would report its opinion back to the House of Burgesses.

"Cousin John?" Maria whispered, beginning to wonder how their petition would be treated.

Cousin John laid a finger across his lips, and Maria was startled into silence as she heard the clerk announce the presentation of a petition from

Clementina Rind, "praying that she may be appointed Printer to the Public, in place of her husband, Mr. William Rind, deceased."

In almost the same breath the clerk offered the petition of Alexander Purdie, printer, for the same, and also the petition of John Dixon for the same. All the petitions were submitted separately, to Maria's surprise, so there were not just two petitions for the government printing. There were three, which made her mother's chances seem even more difficult.

Maria listened as the petitions were read and the order was given that the petitions be taken into consideration on Tuesday, the twenty-fourth day of May.

Counting on her fingers, Maria sighed with frustration. This was only May seventh. May twenty-fourth was seventeen days away!

As the clerk began to present a petition from the upper inhabitants of the County of Stafford, Cousin John led Maria out of the Capitol into the bright sunlight.

"Seventeen days is a long time to wait," Maria complained, but as she spoke she began to see that the wait might be a blessing. Two more issues of her mother's *Gazette* would be published during that time. If her mother would print a few articles favorable to the Crown, then perhaps she *could* win the government printing contract. Why didn't she seem to understand this?

Chapter Eleven

During the next few days, while Maria was out of the house on errands, she kept her eyes and ears open for any newsworthy item that was favorable to the Crown. If only the right story would come along!

It was in John Greenhow's store that Mrs. Miller, of all people, gave Maria the answer.

Mrs. Miller and her husband had been guests at a general entertainment the governor and his lady had given for all city officials. Maria knew that Mr. Miller was a member of the Williamsburg Common Council, and she was sure that the women who were shopping knew this, too. However, Mrs. Miller described the Governor's Palace and the reception as if her husband were a titled lord as well.

"The precious children were exceedingly well-mannered as they greeted us," she said. "They are all studying with dance masters, and the daughters of the family practice daily on the spinet."

"As do the children of our Virginia gentry," a woman near Maria said in a low voice.

Mrs. Miller had heard the remark. With a disdainful look, she said, "But *their* dance master comes from *London.* Virginia children cannot be taught half so well."

She went on to speak of the tasty punch and cakes that had been served, but Maria kept thinking of the children. Her mother could write a poem about these well-bred, well-taught children that would certainly please Lady Dunmore and all who read it. But her mother had already shown a lack of interest in writing about the Dunmore children.

If Mama won't write the poem, Maria thought, *then I shall!* Her unskilled penmanship wouldn't matter because the poem would be set in type.

The next day would be Wednesday, May eighteenth. Maria knew that this was the day on which the type would be set in typestick, moved to a galley, tied with string, made up, and then locked into newspaper-size iron formes. The first forme would be locked into the bed of the printing press. In the morning, all the formes would be ready to print the pages of Thursday's *Gazette.* It would be the last issue that would be printed before the burgesses made their decision. It might be the most important issue her mother had ever published!

That afternoon Maria struggled to write her poem.

Noble children, new to Virginia's shores, she began. She studied the line, wondering, *Is this what Mama would write? Maybe I should add a pleasing compliment.*

Beginning again, Maria wrote: *Noble children, with grace and charm, new to Virginia's shores.*

Better by far, she decided, and worked hard to write the rest of the poem, managing to finish it before it was time to prepare the light evening meal.

In the morning, her poem in her pocket, Maria left Johnny, Charlie, and Jemmy at their play and walked into the printing office. Her mother was bent over her desk, so intent on what she was writing that she didn't see Maria at her side.

"Mama," Maria said. "I wish to ask a favor of you."

Startled, Clementina sat upright, looking at Maria with surprise. "What troubles you?" she asked.

"Nothing troubles me, Mama," Maria answered. "I—I have written a short poem about Lord and Lady Dunmore's children."

Clementina sighed and picked up her quill.

"Daughter, I'm sorry, but I have no time now to listen to your poem."

"I pray you, Mama. It is but a short poem. I will read it to you."

As Maria took a sheet of paper from her pocket and began to unfold it, Clementina spoke sharply. "We have just received word that on March thirty-first, Parliament passed what is called the Boston Port Act. The act ordered that the port of Boston be closed on June first, unless the City of Boston pays for the tea that was destroyed in the harbor last December sixteenth."

Maria remembered how much tea had been pulled from containers on three ships and dumped into Boston Harbor. She couldn't begin to imagine how much it would cost. "How can they pay for all that tea?" she asked.

"That is not the problem," Clementina said. "They *will* not pay it. This retaliation against the Bostonians is intolerable!"

Gulping down the lump of fear that rose in her throat, Maria asked, "Are you going to write about it?"

"Of course," Clementina answered. "It is my job as printer of the *Gazette* to keep our readers informed."

She held up the paper on which she had been writing and said to Maria, "I think this is ready to set in type. I'll read it aloud to make sure there is nothing else I might wish to change."

Maria listened in despair as Clementina read, finishing with, "The illegal and unwarrantable act of Parliament, passed on the thirtieth of March last, and principally against the Bostonians, whose patriotic conduct on so interesting an occasion deserved the highest applause, will not, it is hoped, quell their free spirit, now the storm is beginning, and more especially as there are so many united colonies to protect her at so critical a juncture."

"The storm is beginning," Maria echoed. She could feel the fury of the wind and the chill of the rain as if it tore through her own body. "Oh, Mama, I pray you," she begged, "do what you can to help the storm pass quickly."

Clementina, seemingly intent on her work, didn't answer Maria. She walked to one of the typecases, ready to set her article in type.

Maria followed, more fearful than ever now that she realized how much tomorrow's newspaper could anger some of the *Gazette*'s readers. "Mama," she begged, "pray listen to my poem."

Impatiently, Clementina glanced at Maria as if she'd forgotten she was in the room. "Not now, daughter," she said. "I have work to do, and so do you."

Disappointed, Maria left the pressroom and headed for the outdoor kitchen, where she had to begin preparations for the afternoon meal. Carefully she folded the sheet of paper again and returned it to her pocket. Her mother had dismissed the poem because she had thought it was not important, but Maria knew it was needed to balance her mother's article against King George's actions.

As Maria worked, scrubbing and peeling potatoes and scraping carrots, she began to see a solution to her problem. That night the type for the next day's newspaper would be set, but until it was inked for printing it could be changed, couldn't it?

Her heart began to beat faster with excitement as the idea developed and grew. She had helped sort the type. She knew uppercase from lowercase. She knew that the type was set in a typestick to form words and lines. She had seen Dick do this job over and over again. It looked simple enough. She could do it, too.

What if she were to remove a few lines of type from one of the formes—an advertisement, perhaps—to make room for her poem? Her mother might be upset at first, but surely, when she discovered how well the poem was received by everyone, she would realize that Maria had made a wise choice.

I'll do it! Maria thought. She put down the paring knife and touched her cool fingertips to her burning cheeks. *I'll do it tonight after everyone in the family is asleep.*

That night Maria lay in bed, quilt pulled up to her ears, and waited until the house was silent and her mother's breathing became deep and even. Then she tiptoed out of the room, through the passage, and down the stairs, not daring to light a candle until she reached the hall.

Quietly, in the flickering light, she opened the door to the printing office and stepped inside, going directly to the pressroom in the rear. The huge printing press loomed before her; the forme for pages two and three of the *Gazette* was already locked onto its bed.

The other forme with pages one and four had been washed with lye, then rinsed, and stacked with the type side against the wall to dry. Maria bent over the forme already in the printing press and studied the type, looking for a short item that could be removed. She stared at the type, then squinted. There was something wrong! The letters of the type seemed to be in a jumble. The words made no sense. And the dim light from the flickering candle didn't help.

But as Maria studied the letters, she realized they had been set in reverse order. Of course. The paper would be pressed against the ink on the type, so it would be like holding a paper up to a looking glass. The words would be backward in the chase but be right side around when printed on the paper.

She sighed. This would make her job more difficult. However, she was determined to set her poem in print. There seemed to be nothing she could change on the inside pages of the *Gazette*. She would have to study the type in the forme against the wall.

With difficulty she pulled the heavy forme away from the wall it was leaning on and, balancing it carefully, she tried to make out the backward wording.

There was a short space on the left. She read the top line in reverse, sounding out one word at a time: "To be SOLD, at public auction."

"Very good," Maria whispered to herself. "This announcement for a farmer's livestock to be sold can certainly be removed from the newspaper without loss. My poem has exactly the same number of lines."

If she could manage to carefully lay the forme on the floor and unlock it, so she could remove the lines, she could make the change. Grunting with the effort she was making, Maria slowly began to lower the forme, which she was certain must weigh about sixty pounds.

"What are you doing, child?" Cousin John's voice boomed through the office.

Startled, Maria let out a shriek and dropped the forme. As it fell to the floor with a crash, the loose type scattered.

"Oh!" Maria cried.

Cousin John looked horrified. "What have you done?" he exclaimed.

Clementina, still in her shift, stepped through the doorway. She stopped short, staring at the scattered type. "Maria! What happened?" she gasped.

"Oh, Mama," Maria wailed. "I only wanted to insert my poem in the newspaper. I was trying to take out the type for an item about livestock to be auctioned. I didn't mean to spill the type."

Clementina put her hands on Maria's shoulders. "Stop crying and look at me," she said. "You had no right to remove the advertisement. I accepted payment for it. I have the obligation to print it."

"Oh," Maria managed to say. "I didn't think."

"No, you didn't."

Maria clasped her mother tightly. "Mama," she cried, "I am so afraid that because of the information you put in our newspaper you will lose the government printing contract. And then what will happen to us? We won't have a home! Or beds! Or food!"

Clementina held Maria until the tears had passed.

Then she said, "I will not neglect my family, Maria. I promise you that. But I also will not neglect my duty. I must hold to what I believe. I refuse to be cowardly and compromise my beliefs in an attempt to please everyone. Would you really wish me to do this?"

Maria looked up, shocked. "No, Mama! I would never want you to be a coward!"

"That's what I would be if I did not stand up for what I knew to be right and true." Clementina stroked Maria's damp hair from her forehead as she added, "It was not only Thomas Jefferson, but other burgesses who invited your father to come to Williamsburg to print a newspaper that would bring all sides to the Virginia colonists. Your father was happy to do this, and I have no choice but to continue his work. Do you understand?"

"Yes, Mama," Maria said. "I do. But if it means not being afraid—"

"I did not say that. There are many nights on which I find it hard to sleep and must wrestle with my fears." Clementina smiled. "I can promise you, though, it's easier to be afraid when in your heart you know you are doing what is right."

Cousin John broke into the conversation. "Luckily we've already printed these pages, but all the advertisements that need to appear in the next issue have been pied. If we're to reset them in time to print, we'll need to sort the type tonight."

"We are ready, cousin," Clementina said. She gave Maria a final pat on her shoulder. "Bring more candles, daughter. We have work to do."

Chapter Twelve

On Tuesday, May twenty-fourth, Maria and William, dressed in their best clothes, walked to the Capitol with Clementina and Cousin John in time to be present when the House of Burgesses began the day's session.

Maria was every bit as nervous as she had been on her first visit. She knew now that her mother was right to stand up for what she believed and inform the Virginia colonists of the truth behind every action of both the patriots and the Crown. However, she couldn't help thinking about the uproar her mother's decision to include news about the Boston Port Bill had caused among some of the people in Williamsburg.

Would her mother be awarded the government contract? Or would she not?

Clementina would not speak of the contract, but William had whispered to Maria late one evening that he was very much afraid their mother would lose the contract. Cousin John's serious expression told Maria that he, too, thought the contract might go to Mr. Purdie or Mr. Dixon.

Maria's legs trembled as she neared the Capitol and once more stood under the portico just outside the open doors of the House of Burgesses.

The burgesses had not yet taken their places, and Maria could see small groups of the men chatting among themselves. At one side, however, a cluster of men stood close to each other, speaking earnestly to Robert Carter Nicholas, the treasurer of the Colony and burgess of James City County. Mr. Nicholas was a man whom everyone in Williamsburg knew and respected. He was taking a paper from a man whom Maria recognized as Thomas Jefferson, who had on occasion met with her father. Looking on was Patrick Henry, who was well known throughout Virginia for his outspoken ways. She was fairly sure that the other two men in the group were Richard Henry Lee and Francis Lightfoot Lee.

As the meeting was called to order, Mr. Purdie and Mr. Dixon moved a little closer to the doorway. Maria tried not to look at them. She tried to pretend they weren't even there.

William nudged her and whispered, "Will the burgesses hear Mama's petition now?"

Maria put a finger to her lips, urging him to be quiet, and shook her head. She was so intent on wishing her mother would win the government contract, she had no desire to enjoy feeling superior to William or pointing out that she knew the order of business and he didn't.

Mr. Richard Henry Lee gave a report from the Committee of Courts of Justice on a petition they had studied. A vote was called for, and the petition was rejected.

William gave a nervous gulp so loud in the hall that Maria could hear it. "Shhh!" she whispered.

But William persisted. "Is it our turn now?"

Maria shook her head.

Two other petitions were read by the clerk to the House and were sent to committee.

William's elbow poked Maria's ribs. "Now?" he whispered.

Maria didn't have to answer.

The burgesses became silent as the clerk called out, "The Order of the Day being read, for the House to consider the petition of Clementina Rind, praying that she may be appointed Printer to the Public, in place of her husband, William Rind, deceased. And also the petition of Alexander Purdie, printer, for the same. And also the petition of John Dixon, printer, for the same."

As Mr. Purdie and Mr. Dixon drew even closer to the open doorway, each of the three petitions was read, and it was resolved that the Printer to the Public be chosen by ballot.

Maria's heartbeat quickened. It was hard to breathe as she listened to the Speaker's instructions to members to write their choices on slips of paper and deposit them in glass containers. She wished she could shout, "Vote for my mother! Write her name on your slips of paper!" Instead, she thought the words over and over in her mind.

It seemed to take forever for the clerk and the sergeant-at-arms to collect the papers and place them on the clerk's table. Maria nearly groaned with impatience as a committee was appointed to withdraw from the chamber with the tickets, count them, and report back with the results.

Clementina stood as still as a statue, but her face was pale, and her hand was cold as Maria clutched it. Maria closed her eyes, wondering what might happen to her family. Her mother had to be able to pay for the printing equipment and household furniture she had bought on credit at the sale back in October.

As the clerk called out that the tickets had been counted, Maria opened her eyes with a start. She listened carefully as one of the burgesses reported, "We have examined the ballots accordingly, and the majority falls upon the said Clementina Rind."

"We have won the appointment!" Clementina whispered, and she squeezed Maria's hand so tightly that it hurt.

The burgess loudly announced, "For Clementina Rind, sixty votes. For Alexander Purdie and Mrs. Rind, twenty-five votes. For John Dixon and Mrs. Rind, two votes. Ordered, that the said Clementina Rind be appointed Printer to the Public."

Tears of joy filled Maria's eyes. The vote made it clear that her mother would have shared in the contract had either of the two men won the vote.

"Can we leave now?" William whispered.

But Robert Carter Nicholas stood and announced he wished to introduce a resolution.

"Wait," Clementina whispered in turn. "I want to hear this resolution."

In a clear, strong voice of authority, Mr. Nicholas read the paper Maria had seen Thomas Jefferson give to him. Maria and her mother listened intently, as Mr. Nicholas spoke of great dangers to British America from the hostile invasion of the city of Boston, whose commerce and harbor were, on the first day of June, to be stopped by an armed force from Great Britain.

Mr. Nicholas's voice boomed out as he said, "We deem it highly necessary that the said first day of June be set apart, by the members of this House, as a day of fasting, humiliation, and prayer, devoutly to implore the divine interposition, of averting the heavy calamity which threatens destruction to our civil rights, and the evils of civil war."

Maria was shocked by the words *civil war*. But she had no time to explore the idea because she was caught by other statements Mr. Nicholas read: ". . . to give us one heart and one mind firmly to oppose, by all just and proper means, every injury to American rights" and the plea "that the minds of his Majesty and his Parliament may be inspired from above with wisdom, moderation, and justice, to remove from the loyal people of America all cause of danger."

Maria suddenly realized what her mother had been trying to tell her. It was not only the people of Boston who were in danger. The people of Virginia were, too. The rights of *all* the colonists—"American rights," they were called—were threatened by the acts of the British authorities.

Mr. Nicholas continued to read. The burgesses would walk with the speaker carrying the mace—a ceremonial staff—to Bruton Parish Church at ten o'clock on June first. The Reverend Mr. Price was appointed to read prayers, and the Reverend Mr.

Gwatkin was asked to preach a sermon suitable to the occasion.

Maria could picture in her mind a long, impressive procession of the burgesses and many citizens of Williamsburg willing to go hungry all that day to show their sympathies for their fellow colonists in Massachusetts. Together they would fill the church, beseeching God's assistance and protection. Maybe all the Rinds would walk in the procession—even little Jemmy—and in the following issue of their *Gazette* Mama would write about it.

His voice dropping as he reached the end of the resolution, Mr. Nicholas said, "Ordered, that this resolution be forthwith printed and published."

As the resolution was carried unanimously, with great excitement among the burgesses, Clementina excitedly clasped her hands together and said to Cousin John, "Upon returning home, as government printer, I shall immediately print a broadside to quickly inform our readers. Now that I know we will have our printing equipment for the length of the new contract, I must continue to use it to keep the people of Williamsburg informed."

Maria could hear the relief and enthusiasm in her mother's voice and was proud of all she had achieved.

Over the noise from the chamber, where the

burgesses had left their places and were moving to speak with one another, Cousin John leaned close to Clementina. "But tomorrow is the day we must ready the *Gazette* to be printed," he said.

Maria saw that her mother's back was as straight as a broomstick, and her eyes sparkled with enthusiasm for what the burgesses had just done. "The broadside must come first. Perhaps we'll delay the newspaper until Friday to include the governor's reaction," she said. She lowered her voice so that only her family could hear her. "This resolution for a day of fasting, humiliation, and prayer will anger Lord Dunmore. He will be likely to dissolve the assembly. This is news our readers will want to learn."

"On what grounds will he dissolve the assembly?" Cousin John asked in surprise.

"Lord Dunmore does not usually seek reason for his actions, but I might guess he will say that, as governor, he has the only legal authority to call for days of fasting."

"*Now* will we leave?" William asked impatiently.

"Now," Clementina answered with a smile. With a gracious nod to both Mr. Purdie and Mr. Dixon, Clementina took Maria's hand and left the Capitol.

William waited until he was outside. Then he ran and jumped, let out two loud whoops, and dashed down Duke of Gloucester Street toward home. Cousin John hurried to catch up with Clementina and Maria.

"I will return to the printing office soon," he said, his voice high and almost breathless. "There are some friends I wish to see ... some friends with whom I wish to share the good news."

As Maria scurried to keep pace with her mother, she asked, "Mama, what will happen now?"

Clementina stopped and looked down at Maria. "I will continue my job as both printer of the *Virginia Gazette* and printer of official government documents." She smiled as she added, "Perhaps when we return home you will read the poem you have written to me. Now might be the time to print it in our newspaper."

Maria gave a quick skip of joy, but her smile faded as she asked, "What I meant by my question was, what will happen now to our colony? The Crown is punishing the people of Boston, and you said Lord Dunmore will be angry that the burgesses ordered a day of fasting, humiliation, and prayer in Williamsburg. What will happen, Mama?"

"I cannot give you an answer, child," Clementina replied. "Do you remember when I said that a storm was approaching? We do not know when or if it will arrive. We can only prepare for the day it may come."

Maria nodded and again reached for her mother's warm, comforting hand. Fears came with any storm, but for the moment the future and what it might bring seemed very far away.

Epilogue

As Mrs. Otts ended Maria's story, Chip asked, "Mrs. Rind said she would print a broadside. What's a broadside?"

"It's a sheet of paper printed on just one side," Mrs. Otts explained. "It could be handed out or posted to a wall or a fence. It was a speedy way to get the news of the day of fasting, humiliation, and prayer to the citizens of Williamsburg."

"Was Mrs. Rind right about the resolution making Lord Dunmore angry?" Keisa asked.

"Yes, indeed," Mrs. Otts answered. "Considering Lord Dunmore's previous actions, that was easy for her to predict. Two days later, on Thursday, he summoned the House of Burgesses to attend him in the council chamber. He held up a printed version of the resolution—perhaps one printed by Clementina Rind—and angrily announced that the contents reflected negatively upon King George III and the Parliament of Great Britain. Therefore, he found it necessary to dissolve the House of Burgesses immediately."

"That means they couldn't meet anymore. Right?" Halim asked.

Mrs. Otts smiled. "Officially, perhaps, but they did meet. They simply moved from the Capitol to the Raleigh Tavern to consider a proposition from Boston that all trade with England cease. Then when the Virginia convention met in August, they decided to forbid the importation of British goods and slaves beginning in November."

Lori spoke up. "There was something else they did—something even more important. We learned in our history class that they elected seven delegates to represent Virginia in the first Continental Congress."

"That's right," said Mrs. Otts. "Patrick Henry, George Washington, and Peyton Randolph were among them."

"They didn't know it, but they were moving closer and closer to war," Keisha said.

"We call it the Revolutionary War, but they called it a *civil* war," Stewart said.

"It was both," Mrs. Otts told him. "It would be a

war in which families would be painfully divided. Some held tightly to their British citizenship. Others yearned for the promise of a free nation. There were even families of patriots in which fathers urged care and caution but sons were heedless of this advice and yearned for action."

She paused. "Like the Robert Carter Nicholas family."

"He was the one who introduced the resolution for fasting, humiliation, and prayer," Lori said.

" 'Tis true," Mrs. Otts said. "The resolution had been written by Thomas Jefferson, Patrick Henry, George Mason, and the Lees, but they urged Mr. Nicholas to read it to the burgesses because people respected what has been called his 'grave and religious character.' Historians believe that Mr. Nicholas was cautious and moderate at that time just in hope that matters would be set right and there would be relief from wrongs and injuries. After another year had passed, however, he had to contend with his son George."

Chip asked, "Was George just a kid? What did he do?"

"George was not a child. He was a young man of twenty when he was involved in a number of wild and dangerous escapades. But it was not just George that Mr. Nicholas was worried about. It was also his son John, who was only eleven, but who was trying to follow his big brother's lead. I recall the time when John and his best friend, Robert Waller, sneaked from their homes in the dark of night, and could have been killed when . . ."

She stopped. "Ah, but there's much more to John's story than that terrible night that frightened everyone in Williamsburg."

Lori bounced up and down. "Tell us John's story! Please, Mrs. Otts?"

"Yes, please!" Keisha begged. "Our class's field trip is over tomorrow, and we don't want to miss hearing your story about John."

"Very well," Mrs. Otts said, nodding. "Meet with me this evening and I'll tell you all about John Nicholas and what happened to change his life in the year 1775."

Author's Note

I wrote Maria Rind's story with a touch of sadness.
As I researched her life, she came to life for me—a
sweet, serious girl who did what was asked of her
and did it well.

Because of their circumstances, Maria's mother
had little time to teach her either the household
chores girls traditionally learned from their mothers,
or skills in reading and writing. The historians at the
Colonial Williamsburg Foundation have a letter
written by Maria as an adult, and it shows that her
penmanship was poor. She still crossed out words,
wrote in uneven lines, and was guilty of a few
inkblots. My heart went out to Maria. Although she
wished so eagerly to learn, she was limited to what
she could teach herself.

Maria's parents seemed to have been kind and loving, and she had been close to them, so I knew how terribly hard it must have been for her to lose her father.

But much more sorrow was in store for Maria.

Her mother worked hard to make the business prosper. Clementina Rind also sold books, set up a post office in her printing office, and even took in a few boarders. Courageously, over the next four months, Clementina printed news articles, broadsides, and pamphlets with colonial grievances in mind, helping to ready Virginians for the "approaching storm."

Thomas Jefferson had drafted proposed instructions to the Virginia delegation to the colonists' convention in Philadelphia. Although the convention did not accept them, friends had the instructions published in August 1774 by Clementina Rind, calling the pamphlet *A Summary of the Rights of British America.*

It must have been a terrible shock for Maria and her brothers when, only four months after winning the government printing contract, their mother's health deteriorated. Clementina Rind died on September 25, 1774.

Cousin John Pinkney attempted to take over the printing business and support the children. In May

1775, he applied for the position of Printer to the Public, but Alexander Purdie won the appointment instead.

John Pinkney did his best to continue to care for the Rind orphans, but the business quickly fell even deeper into debt—probably for a number of reasons. He no longer received the salary given for government printing; he was accused of poor business management, and I am guessing that he could not equal Clementina's skills. John Pinkney died in 1776, leaving the Rind children to be cared for by the community.

We know that the Masonic Lodge of Williamsburg, of which Maria's father had been a member, set aside money for the boarding, schooling, and clothing of William and John. William grew up to become a printer and published the *Virginia Federalist* in Richmond from 1799 to 1800. He then moved to Georgetown in the District of Columbia to publish the *Washington Federalist*.

James, the youngest of the Rind children, became a lawyer in Richmond. We have no information about John's occupation as an adult, and there is no record of Charles, so historians think he may have died while still a child.

Maria was not cared for as well as her brothers. She was bound out—that is, obliged to work as a servant—to a family whose name is not known. In 1777, Sarah Norton, a daughter of Robert Carter Nicholas, discovered how Maria was being neglected. She asked her friend Frances Randolph to take Maria into her household, and Frances did, happily treating Maria like one of the family.

The next year, Frances married St. George Tucker, and Maria lived with them, caring for their children and doing a few of the household chores as well. In 1791, when Maria was twenty-seven, she married John Coalter (later to become a judge), who at the time was tutor for the Tucker children. Sadly, the next year Maria died in childbirth.

Sarah Hay, who was Maria's best friend in this story, married Henry Nicholson, also of Williamsburg, when she was grown. Records show they had four children.

Burgesses who wrote the resolution to call for a day of fasting, humiliation, and prayer spoke of civil war in 1774, but few imagined it would come to that in two short years.

As I planned my story, I had to imagine what Maria would have done in these troublesome times. Clementina had made the most of Lady Dunmore's arrival in Williamsburg. Perhaps Maria actually had encouraged her mother to do so. I was fairly certain that she would have worried that enough burgesses would give full support to the King and Parliament to cause her mother to lose the government contract and the salary that came with it. If that happened, she would be unable to support her family. Clementina Rind and John Pinkney might have been more confident than I made them appear, but under such trying circumstances I believe they both had plenty of cause for worry.

In my story, Maria came to support wholeheartedly her mother's courageous actions in writing the truth about what the British authorities were doing. However, these were fearful times, and I knew that no matter how strongly Maria stood for truth and freedom, she would have been afraid.

Anyone who lived at this time, as disagreement and suspicion grew between England and her colonies, would have been afraid, too. They knew they had no choice but to prepare for the approaching storm.

About
Williamsburg

The story of Williamsburg, the capital of eighteenth-century Virginia, began more than seventy-five years before the thirteen original colonies became the United States in 1776.

Williamsburg was the colony's second capital. Jamestown, the first permanent English settlement in North America, was the first. Jamestown stood on a swampy peninsula in the James River, and over the years, people found it an unhealthy place to live. They also feared that ships sailing up the river could attack the town.

In 1699, a year after the Statehouse at Jamestown burned down for the fourth time, Virginians decided to move the capital a few miles away, to a place known

The Capitol at Williamsburg

as Middle Plantation. On high ground between two rivers, Middle Plantation was a healthier and safer location that was already home to several of Virginia's leading citizens.

Middle Plantation was also the home of the College of William and Mary, today one of Virginia's most revered institutions. The college received its charter from King William III and Queen Mary II of England in 1693. Its graduates include two of our nation's first presidents: Thomas Jefferson and James Monroe.

The new capital's name was changed to Williamsburg in honor of King William. Like the Colony of Virginia, Williamsburg grew during the eighteenth century. Government officials and their families arrived. Taverns opened for business, and merchants and artisans settled in. Much of the heavy labor and domestic work was performed by African Americans, most of them slaves, although a few were free. By the eve of the American Revolution, nearly two thousand people—roughly half of them white and half of them black—lived in Williamsburg.

The Revolutionary War and Its Leaders

The formal dates of the American Revolution are 1775 to 1783, but the problems between the thirteen original colonies and Great Britain, their mother country, began in 1765, when Parliament enacted the Stamp Act.

England was in debt from fighting the Seven Years War (called the French and Indian War in the colonies) and believed that the colonists should help pay the debt. The colonists were stunned. They considered themselves English and believed they had the same political rights as people living in England. These rights included being taxed *only* by an elected body, such as each colony's legislature. Now a body in which they were not represented, Parliament, was taxing them.

A reenactment of Virginia legislators debating the Stamp Act

All thirteen colonies protested, and the Stamp Act was repealed in 1766. Over the next nine years, however, Great Britain imposed other taxes and enacted other laws that the colonists believed infringed on their rights. Finally, in 1775, the second Continental Congress, made up of representatives from twelve of the colonies, established an army. The following year, the Congress (now with representatives from all thirteen colonies) declared independence from Great Britain.

The Revolutionary War was the historical event that ensured Williamsburg's place in American history. Events that happened there and the people who participated in them helped form the values on which the United States was founded. Virginians meeting in Williamsburg helped lead the thirteen colonies to independence.

In fact, Americans first declared independence in the Capitol building in Williamsburg. There, on May 15, 1776, the colony's leaders declared Virginia's full freedom from England. In a unanimous vote, they also instructed the colony's representatives to the Continental Congress to propose that the Congress "declare the United Colonies free and independent states absolved from all allegiances to or dependence upon the Crown or Parliament of Great Britain."

Three weeks later, Richard Henry Lee, one of Virginia's delegates, stood before the Congress and proposed independence. His action led directly to the writing of the Declaration of Independence. The Congress adopted the Declaration on July 2 and signed it two days later. The United States of America was born.

Williamsburg served as a training ground for

three noteworthy patriots: George Washington, Thomas Jefferson, and Patrick Henry. Each arrived in Williamsburg as a young man, and there each matured into a statesman.

In 1752, George Washington, who later led the American forces to victory over the British in the Revolutionary War and became our nation's first president, came to Williamsburg at the age of nineteen. He soon began a career in the military, which led to a seat in Virginia's legislature, the House of Burgesses. He served as a burgess for sixteen years—negotiating legislation, engaging in political discussions, and building social and political relationships. These experiences helped mold him into one of America's finest political leaders.

Patrick Henry, who would go on to become the first governor of the Commonwealth of Virginia as well as a powerful advocate for the Bill of Rights, first traveled to Williamsburg in 1760 to obtain a law license. Only twenty-three years old, he barely squeaked through the exam. Five years later, as a first-time burgess, he led Virginia's opposition to the Stamp Act. For the next eleven years, Henry's talent as a speaker—including his now famous Caesar-Brutus speech and the immortal cry, "Give me liberty or give me death!"—rallied Virginians to the patriots' cause.

Thomas Jefferson, who later wrote the Declaration of Independence, succeeded Patrick Henry as the governor of Virginia, and became the third president of the United States, arrived in Williamsburg in 1760 at the age of seventeen to attend the College of William and Mary. As the cousin of Peyton Randolph, the respected Speaker of the House of Burgesses, Jefferson was immediately welcomed by Williamsburg society. He became a lawyer and was elected a burgess in 1769. In his very first session, the royal governor closed the legislature because it had protested the Townshend Acts. The burgesses moved the meeting to the Raleigh Tavern, where they drew up an agreement to boycott British goods.

Jefferson, Henry, and Washington each signed the agreement. In the years that followed, all three men supported the patriots' cause and the nation that grew out of it.

Williamsburg Then and Now

Williamsburg in the eighteenth century was a vibrant American town. Thanks largely to the vision of the Reverend Dr. W.A.R. Goodwin, rector of Bruton Parish Church at the opening of the twentieth century, its vitality can still be experienced today. The generosity of philanthropist John D. Rockefeller, Jr., made it possible to restore Williamsburg to its eighteenth-century glory. Original colonial buildings

The Reverend Dr. W.A.R. Goodwin with John D. Rockefeller, Jr.

were acquired and carefully returned to their eighteenth-century appearance. Later houses and buildings were torn down and replaced by carefully researched reconstructions, most built on original eighteenth-century foundations. Rockefeller gave the project both money and enthusiastic support for more than thirty years.

Today, the Historic Area of Williamsburg is both a museum and a living city. The restored buildings, antique furnishings, and costumed interpreters can help you create a picture of the past in your mind's eye. The Historic Area is operated by the Colonial Williamsburg Foundation, a nonprofit educational organization staffed by historians, interpreters, actors, administrators, numerous people behind the scenes, and many volunteers.

Williamsburg is a living reminder of our country's past and a guide to its future; it shows us where we have been and can give us clues about where we may be going. Though the stories of the people who lived in the eighteenth-century Williamsburg may seem very different from our lives in the twenty-first century, the heart of the stories remains the same. We created a nation based on new ideas about liberty, independence, and democracy. The Colonial Williamsburg: Young Americans books are about individuals who may not have experienced these principles in their own lives, but whose lives foreshadowed changes for the generations that followed. People like the smart and capable Ann McKenzie in *Ann's Story: 1747,* who struggled to reconcile her interest in medicine with society's expectations for an eighteenth-century woman. People like the brave Caesar in *Caesar's Story: 1759,* who struggled in silence against the institution of slavery that gripped his people, his family, and himself. While some of these lives evoke painful memories of

A scene from Colonial Williamsburg today

our country's history, they are a part of that history nonetheless and cannot be forgotten. These stories form the foundation of our country. The people in them are the unspoken heroes of our time.

Childhood in Eighteenth-Century Virginia

If you traveled back in time to Virginia in the 1700s, some things would probably seem familiar to you. Colonial children played some of the same games that children play today: blindman's buff, hopscotch, leapfrog, and hide-and-seek. Girls had dolls, boys flew kites, and both boys and girls might play with puzzles and read.

You might be surprised, however, at how few toys even well-to-do children owned. Adults and children in the 1700s owned far fewer things than we do today, not only fewer toys but also less furniture and clothing. And the books children read were either educational or taught them how to behave properly, such as *Aesop's Fables* and the *School of Manners*.

Small children dressed almost alike back then. Boys and girls in prosperous families wore gowns  (dresses) similar to the ones older girls and women wore. Less well-to-do white children and enslaved children wore shifts, which were much like our nightgowns. Both black and white boys began wearing pants when they were between five and seven years old.

Boys and girls in colonial Virginia began doing chores when they were six or seven, probably the same age at which *you* started doing chores around the house. But their chores included tasks such as toting kindling, grinding corn with a mortar and pestle, and turning a spit so that meat would roast evenly over the fire.

These chores were done by both black and white children. Many enslaved children also began working in the fields at this age. They might pick worms off tobacco, carry water to older workers, hoe, or pull weeds. However, they usually were not expected to do as much work as the adults.

As black and white children grew older, they were assigned more and sometimes harder chores. Few children of either race went to school. Those who did usually came from prosperous white families, although there were some charity schools. Some middling (middle-class) and gentry (upper-class) children studied at home with tutors. Other white children learned from their mothers and fathers to read, write, and do simple arithmetic. But not all white children were taught these skills, and very few enslaved children learned them.

When they were ten, eleven, or twelve years old, children began preparing in earnest for adulthood.

Boys from well-to-do families got a university education at the College of William and Mary in Williamsburg or at a university in England. Their advanced studies prepared them to manage the plantations they inherited or to become lawyers and important government officials. Many did all three things.

Many middle-class boys and some poorer ones became apprentices. An apprentice agreed to work for a master for several years, usually until the apprentice turned twenty-one. The master agreed to teach the apprentice his trade or profession, to ensure that he learned to read and write, and, usually, to feed, clothe,

An apprentice with the master cabinetmaker

and house him. Apprentices became apothecaries (druggist-doctors), blacksmiths, carpenters, coopers (barrel makers), founders (men who cast metals in a foundry), merchants, printers, shoemakers, silver-smiths, store clerks, and wigmakers. Some girls, usually orphans with no families, also became apprentices. A girl apprentice usually lived with a family and worked as a domestic servant.

Most white girls, however, learned at home. Their mothers or other female relatives taught them the skills they would need to manage their households after they married—such as cooking, sewing, knitting, cleaning, doing the laundry, managing domestic slaves, and caring for ailing family members. Some middle-class and most gentry girls also learned music, dance, embroidery, and sometimes French. Formal education for girls of all classes, however, was usually limited to reading, writing, and arithmetic.

Enslaved children also began training for adulthood when they were ten to twelve years old. Some boys and girls worked in the house and learned to be domestic slaves. Others worked in the fields. Some boys learned a trade.

Because masters had to pay taxes on slaves who were sixteen years old or older, slaves were expected to do a full day's work when they turned sixteen, if not sooner. White boys, however, usually were not considered adults until they reached the age of twenty-one. White girls were considered to be adults when they turned twenty-one or married, whichever came first.

Enslaved or free black boys watching tradesmen saw wood

When we look back, we see many elements of colonial childhood that are familiar to us—the love of toys and games, the need to help the family around the house, and the task of preparing for adulthood. However, it is interesting to compare the days of a colonial child to the days of a child today, and to see all the ways in which life has changed for children over the years.

Printing in Eighteenth-Century Virginia

In eighteenth-century Virginia, printing offices were the communications hubs of the colony. Printers produced and sold newspapers, political pamphlets, and manuals, which played a key role in spreading news and influencing the decisions the Virginians made during the years before the American Revolution.

Clementina Rind (1740–1774) contributed to the great information explosion of the eighteenth century as editor of the *Virginia Gazette* from 1773 to 1774. She also sold books, pamphlets, and other printed pieces and was elected the official printer for the government. She was the first—and only—woman to operate such an enterprise in the colony.

161

Printing required many different skills. Colonial printers needed both strong minds and strong backs. To set type, they needed to read well and to have good hand-eye coordination. Printers kept the lead letters, or characters, in sectioned wooden cases, with capital (uppercase) letters organized in the trays above the small (lowercase) letters and the blank pieces of lead that made the spaces between the words. They rapidly plucked the tiny lead slabs from the trays to build each word, then each sentence, then each paragraph in a hand-held tool called a type stick.

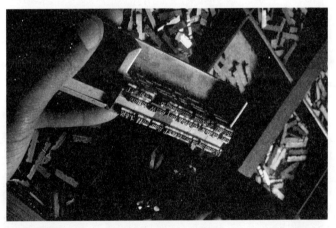

A printer places characters in the type stick.

As the lines of letters to be printed grew, the printers transferred them to a tray called a galley, and then to an imposing table, where it was locked up in an iron frame called a chase. The filled chase made up the forme. Safely on the press bed, the forme was adjusted to produce as uniform an impression as possible. For the *Virginia Gazette,* formes for two newspaper pages were prepared on the press, although only one page could be printed at a time. For an eighteenth-century newspaper like Clementina Rind's *Virginia Gazette,* typesetting required thirty to forty hours of labor for each four-page issue.

To operate the press, printers worked in teams, just as Cousin John and Dick did in Clementina Rind's pressroom. One person was the puller, who

A printer pulls the bar.

positioned the paper and operated the bar; the other was the beater, who inked the type. The puller drew the bar toward him or her, screwing down the platen, or flat plate, which pressed the paper against the inked type below. A colonial puller might pull the bar once every ten seconds, three hundred sixty times per hour, for perhaps fourteen hours per day if the print job required it. Such grueling work required a strong back and focused teamwork to maintain a smooth rhythm.

After accurately printing both sides of the sheet, printers hung the damp sheets from cords near the ceiling to dry. At the end of a long, hard day, printers folded and assembled the dried, printed sheets for distribution to customers. A similar process was used for printing proclamations and other official papers.

Once dry, proclamations and theater bills are publicly posted.

In colonial times, a young man such as William Rind received training during a long apprenticeship to reach the level of journeyman printer. To become a master printer was quite difficult compared with learning other trades. A master printer owned a printing shop and all the equipment in it, which required a far greater investment than most other trades. Such a master had to be shrewd in business matters to run a successful shop in eighteenth-century Virginia.

Colonial Williamsburg Staff

Recipe for Cranberry-Orange Relish

(makes 3 cups)

Maria Rind made cranberry-orange relish to complement the goose served at her family's Christmas dinner. Relishes are flavorful accompaniments to main dishes. With help from an adult, you can make cranberry-orange relish the day before a special meal using the following recipe.

2 cups cranberries
1 orange, quartered and seeded
½ lemon, seeded
1 cup sugar
1 cup pecans

About the
Author

Joan Lowery Nixon is the acclaimed author of more than a hundred books for young readers. She has served as president of the Mystery Writers of America and as regional vice-president for the Southwest Chapter of that society. She is the only four-time winner of the Edgar Allan Poe Best Juvenile Mystery Award given by the Mystery Writers of America and is also a two-time winner of the Golden Spur Award for best juvenile Western, for two of the novels in her Orphan Train Adventures series.

Joan Lowery Nixon and her husband live in Houston.

In the bowl of a food processor, combine the cranberries, orange, and lemon and process until coarsely chopped. Add the sugar and pecans and pulse briefly to mix. Cover and refrigerate overnight.

From *The Colonial Williamsburg Tavern Cookbook*, published by Clarkson Potter in association with the Colonial Williamsburg Foundation